Harriet
the
Horrible

Harriet
the
Horrible

E.R.Reilly

FIRST
STEP

PUBLISHED IN GREAT BRITAIN BY
FIRST STEP
PO BOX 8808
BIRMINGHAM
B30 2LR
E-mail (for orders and enquiries: firststep@reilly19.freeserve.co.uk

First published in 2000
Reprinted 2001, 2002, 2003

Illustrations © Jane Dix 2000

ISBN 0-9539229-0-1

Printed and bound in India at OM Books, Secunderabad 500055
Email: publisher@ombooks.org | website: www.ombooks.org

Harriet is an intelligent child, but then all children are intelligent.
This book is dedicated to intelligent children everywhere – may your intelligence be recognised

Acknowledgements

Books never come to fruition in isolation. This one certainly didn't. I would like to thank Jean Maund for her friendship and close assistance throughout. This book would never have seen the light of day without her technical wizardry, professional commitment and her boundless good humour and encouragement. I would also like to thank Jane Dix for the illustrations and Marion Sacharin who painstakingly checked every detail of the text. Thank you for helping to bring Harriet to life.

Chapter One

You wouldn't want to meet Harriet the Horrible. Everybody thought that Harriet was a lovely little girl. She was a kind of teacher's pet. She was clever, hard working and very polite.

Harry's metamorphosis started one day when her mum told her that they were going to have to move house. This also meant that Harry would have to move school. She was very settled where she was and didn't much like the idea of moving at all.

Harry's teacher, Miss Short, was upset to find out that she was leaving school, and was further upset to find out that she was leaving that very day. Her teacher asked her why she was leaving in such a hurry, but Harry couldn't answer. Harry had asked her mum, but her mum wouldn't give a reason. She just said that they had to leave and that they had to leave straight away and that was that.

Miss Short was so upset that she decided to pay a visit to Harry's mum. She wanted to explain that Harry was very settled where she was and that a sudden change, like moving house and school, would upset her and that it could have a bad effect on her schoolwork.

She was quite surprised when she arrived at the house where Harry lived with her mum. In the front garden there was a sink, a broken down car, some old wet newspapers and some black bags of rubbish that had obviously been torn apart by local dogs. Harry's teacher peered through the window and she could see that there was just as much rubbish in the house as there was in the garden. This was not at all how she had expected Harry's house to be. Harry was such a well turned-out little girl. Her school uniform was always neatly pressed and her schoolwork was beautiful.

Miss Short knocked and waited but there was no reply. Eventually, a window opened

from upstairs. It was Harry's mum. She was quite rude to Miss Short. Although Harry's teacher tried to explain how important it was for Harry to stay where she was settled, it was no use. Harry's mum said that she had to go and that was that.

Miss Short felt ever so sorry for Harry and when she returned to school, she told her what had happened. Harry was mortified. She told her teacher that she never should have done that without asking. Harry stamped her foot and folded her arms. Her teacher was rather surprised to see this as she had never seen Harry behave in such a way before.

Harry's teacher gave her a letter. In it, she had written her address and her phone number. She told Harry to get in touch with her if she ever wanted a chat. Harry took the letter but she was very unhappy. She didn't smile and she didn't even say goodbye properly.

Later that day, Harry gathered her favourite things together and left in a taxi for the train station. She quizzed her mum, asking her why they had to leave in such a hurry, but her mum still wouldn't say. She just said that they had to leave and that was that.

Harry's new flat was an upstairs part of a Victorian house. It wasn't as big as their old house, but it did have a proper garden with a fence. When they arrived, Harry had to go to the garage on the corner and buy some tea and milk. Then, she had to make the tea, whilst her mum lay on the settee and had a rest. Harry was used to that kind of thing. It was the way it had been ever since she could remember.

Harry's new school was all right, but it wasn't the same as being with her old friends and her old teacher. Her new teacher was a little man with bony fingers and glasses that were too big for his head. He kept pointing at Harry and looking at her over his glasses. She didn't like him at all.

Harry didn't like the children in the new class either. They were nasty to her and they called her names. They teased her about her accent because it was different to theirs. They had a gang and the gang members naturally picked on anyone who wasn't in their gang. Harry had heard that the gang met down by the river after school and one of their favourite tricks was to push children into it. Harry had to walk a long way home just to avoid them. Harry was more concerned than most children about keeping her uniform neat and tidy because she did all of her own washing and ironing whilst her mum lay on the settee, and so she certainly wanted to avoid being pushed in the water.

The one good thing about their new home was that it was near the seaside. In fact, it was a bit like being on holiday at first. Harry and her mum used to go and lie on the beach at weekends. The other people who lived there didn't bother much. They just took the beach for granted.

Harry and her mum were wandering round the shops one day when Harry spotted something that caught her eye. It was a packet of itching powder. Harry stroked her chin. A wonderfully wicked plan came into her mind.

There was a boy at school who was the leader of the gang. His name was Jake, and he bullied Harry and got other children to bully her as well. Harry bought the itching powder and bided her time until the moment was right for revenge.

Their teacher was called Mr Blowitt. The children called him 'Old Snot Nose' behind his back. Mr Blowitt made the children do lots of running in PE lessons. He liked to get the children really tired out. It was during a PE lesson that Harry decided to get her own back on Jake. Before the lesson, Harry sneaked into the class and poured the itching powder into his shorts. She sprinkled some on his vest and in his trainers. She stroked her chin again. It was time for her wonderfully wicked plan.

When the children discovered what she had done to Jake, he would be the laughing stock of the class. In fact, he would be the laughing stock of the whole school. Harry would become the most popular girl in the school, with everyone except Jake, and she didn't care about him anyway.

Mr Blowitt got all the children to do stretches and to jump up and down at the start of the lesson. Harry became a little disappointed. It didn't look as though her plan was going to work. Soon though, a delicious smile spread across her face as the itching powder began to do its work. The class bully started rolling his shoulders and scratching his neck. Then he started scratching his back and pulling the most peculiar faces. Mr Blowitt told him to stand still, but he couldn't. He thought he felt something tickling in his sock, so he started scratching his foot. Mr Blowitt asked him if he had ants in his pants. All the other children started laughing. Then it occurred to him that he might have ants. So he kicked off his shoes and socks. Mr Blowitt told him to stop it at once. He was making an exhibition of himself. But he couldn't stop. In fact, he got worse. He started jumping up and down and screaming, "Help! Help!" he said, "I've got ants in my pants. Help! Help!" He jumped up and down and hopped around the room. He pulled his vest off and shouted some more.

"Help! Somebody help me. I've got ants in my pants! Help! Help! Somebody help!"

Harry loved it. Everybody was pointing at Jake and laughing. Then he started scratching his bum.

"Oh no!" he said, "I've got ants and they're in *my* pants!"

Then he pulled his shorts off and threw them in the air. The children were all falling about laughing at him. Just then, the head teacher walked in and asked what all the commotion was about. When she saw Jake dancing in his underpants, her eyes nearly popped out of her head.

"What on earth is going on?" she asked. She heard a voice running off into the distance shouting, "Help! Help! My bum's on fire."

He ran out of the hall and into the playground. All of the children ran to the window to look at him. He ran over to the pond and sat in it.

"Ahhh!" he said, "That feels better!"

Harry told all of the children what she had done and they gave her three cheers. She was right. It did make her popular. She stroked her chin again. She liked being popular and she liked getting equal. She went home contented that day.

Nice little Harriet had been left behind
and Harriet the Horrible had been born!

Chapter Two

Harry liked her new status. She no longer had to walk the long way home. She had earned the respect of the school gang. Nobody would think of throwing her into the river now, because she was too well liked.

One evening when Harry was walking home from school she was asked if she wanted to join the gang. Harry had never been in a gang before, but then, she had never actually been asked to join a gang before. She thought it over for a while and soon decided that she would join their gang. It was the kind of thing that the old Harriet would never have done, but it was just the kind of thing that Harriet the Horrible would do.

The next day Harry walked down by the river and told them that she would join their gang. It was then that they told her about the initiation ceremony. Before she would be allowed to join, she would have to throw a younger child into the river. They warned her, though, that the teachers and the parents at the school became very angry when a young child was thrown in the river. Harry said that she would have to think about it.

That night, when she was cooking tea, Harry began to think about the initiation ceremony. She didn't mind picking on that bully, Jake. He had picked on enough people in his time, so he deserved it. She didn't like the idea of picking on younger kids, though. She decided to think of a wonderfully wicked plan so that she could get out of the initiation ceremony and still join the gang.

At Harry's new school, most of the children wore school uniform. Sometimes though, children turned up in ordinary clothes and nothing much was said to them. The next day, Harry wore an old tracksuit to school. When she arrived at the river on the way home, the children asked her if she was going to do the initiation ceremony. She told them she was going to do something even better. She said that she was going to throw herself in and have a good old splash about in the water. The kids in the gang didn't believe her. They told her that the river was out of bounds and that nobody was allowed to go near it, let alone in it. Harry said that she would do it anyway if she could join the gang. The gang got into a huddle and quickly agreed. Without any more ado, Harry took a run and jumped with a mighty splash into the water. Then she opened up her school bag and took out a piece of paper. She called out to the kids on the side, "This is what I think of school rules and of Old Snot Nose." Then she blew a big raspberry into the paper and threw it into the water. All of the children on the side cheered and then they started chanting her name.

"Harry! Harry! Harry!"

One by one, Harry took other pieces of paper out of her bag. She screwed them up and threw them into the water. The children gave a bigger cheer with every piece she threw. Then she tipped her bag upside down and emptied the whole bag of papers into the water. The children roared her on. Harry jumped up and down and splashed about in the water. Then one of the boys joined her, then another, and then another. Then one of the girls jumped in and started splashing about. Soon the whole gang was in the water. They were wringing out their school jumpers and throwing their homework away.

The following morning was a special one at their school. There were about twenty irate parents outside the Head Teacher's office. They could be heard shouting from all the way down the corridor.

"My child has got a dreadful cold," said one.

"My child was wet through. We could wring her knickers out when she got home!" yelled another.

"All of my child's homework is floating down the river," shouted yet another angry parent.

They were all asking the poor Head Teacher what she was going to do about it. She told them all how sorry she was and how nothing like that had ever happened in all her years of experience.

"Oh dear me," she said. "What am I going to do? I don't know what to do. What can I do?"

Harry listened from around the corner. She was stroking her chin. She loved it when a plan worked quite as well as this.

Harry decided that this was definitely the school for her. She was happy here. The first thing that Harry did when she joined the gang was to change the initiation ceremony. In future, anybody who wanted to join would have to throw an older child into the water, and it had to be someone who had done something against a gang member. Harry liked this initiation ceremony much better.

One day, shortly after the river incident, Harry was settling down for a nice daydream during a maths lesson when her mum burst into the classroom. She called out to Mr Blowitt,

"Sorry, Mr Snot Nose, but I need to take Harriet out of school."

All of the children laughed. Harry told her that this was not his real name, but she only said,

"Well, I'm sorry, Mr Whatsyourname, but I've still got to take Harriet out of your school."

Harry asked what the matter was and her mum said they were leaving again and that was that. Harry's mum had a rucksack on her back that was stuffed with clothes. She had two black bin liners and a holdall that had clothes and everything she could carry in it.

Harry asked if she could go home and make sure that she had everything that she needed, but her mum said that she couldn't.

Again, Harry asked her mum why they were leaving in such a hurry but her mum said that they just were and that was that.

Mr Blowitt said that he must object. He said that this was all very irregular. Harry's mum said that he could object all he wanted but they were still going.

Harry said goodbye to her friends and they each hugged her, one by one. They were really sorry to see her go. Nobody had been as much fun as she had. Even Jake shook her hand. They had become friendly since Harry had taught him the error of his ways.

Harry and her mum caught a bus, then a coach, and then another bus. Their new flat was in a high-rise block. The lifts didn't work and there was graffiti everywhere. There seemed to be more children running about than could possibly fit in all of the flats. There was a peculiar smell on the stairs as well.

On Harry's floor there was a family with more than its fair share of children. There seemed to be a never-ending supply of children with dirty faces walking in and out of that flat. Some of them called her names and teased her a bit. Harry just smiled to herself and stroked her chin. She thought that they would be making a mistake if they were to make an enemy of Harriet the Horrible. Harry unpacked the clothes and made a cup of tea. She didn't like being on the run, but at least she was more used to it now.

That night, she lay in bed and had a good long read of her book. From time to time, she stopped reading and just lay with her hands behind her head, wondering what her new school would be like.

Chapter Three

As it turned out, Harry's new school wasn't too bad. The children made a bit of a fuss of her. It was strange, but the whole class seemed quite nice. Harry hadn't had much luck with teachers since she left Miss Short, but her new teacher seemed quite nice. In fact, her new teacher spoke with a similar accent to Harry. It was nice not being the only stranger.

Things were not quite so rosy at home. There were dozens of kids roaming around her new estate. Most of them seemed to be the Fitzpatricks, who lived in her block of flats. Harry tried to count them. She thought that there were about twelve of them, all living in a three bedroomed flat. They ruled the roost a bit. On their own they weren't so brave or loud, but together they could shout insults at people and, because there were so many of them, there was nothing that the other kids on the estate could do about it.

Once or twice, when Harry was walking up the stairs to her flat, some of the Fitzpatricks would bump into her on purpose. Harry bided her time. She knew that one day she would find a way to get even. It was a mistake to make an enemy of Harriet the Horrible.

School actually became quite pleasant. She loved reading to her new teacher. It was a real treat to be able to talk about all of the books that she was reading. Most teachers hadn't even read the books that Harry had. When they listened to her read, Harry could tell that they were thinking of something else. They only really concentrated on the children who couldn't read properly. They just gave you a sticker and told you that you were a really good reader. Her new teacher was different, though. She seemed interested in what Harry had to say. It was nice to be listened to and Harry liked her new teacher a lot.

Harry still had the problem of the Fitzpatricks, though. They needed pulling down a peg or two.

Harry noticed a girl who lived on their estate who always seemed to be by herself. One day, Harry saw her sitting on the climbing bars in the play area. She was crying. Harry went over to her and asked her what was wrong. It turned out that the other children on the estate called her "lonely girl" or "lonely". Her real name was Samantha, or Sam for short. Harry said that she would call her Sam. Harry put her hand out and the two girls shook hands.

Sam was quite fat and, because of this, other kids teased her and didn't want to be her friend. Harry knew what it was like to be different. She was a stranger everywhere she went.

Sam was particularly sad on this day because the Fitzpatricks had stolen the new electronic game that her grandmother had bought for her. She knew it had been a lot of money for her grandmother to find. She knew it was the Fizpatricks who had stolen it because they were always pestering her for a go. She'd promised her parents that she wouldn't lend it to anyone.

That morning, she had realised that her game had gone missing. She had asked the Fitzpatricks, but they said they knew nothing about it. The only one they knew about was their own, which just happened to be exactly the same as Sam's.

Harry told Sam not to worry. She said that she would find a way to get even. After all, she thought to herself, if you cross Harriet the Horrible's friends then you cross Harriet herself. And now Sam was her friend. Harry stroked her chin. She thought it was time for another wonderfully wicked plan.

That night Harry went about her usual business. She did her homework, made a meal for herself and her mum, did the vacuuming and all the washing up. All the time, she was dreaming up wonderfully wicked plans. She knew that she needed to get Sam her game back. She needed to give the Fitzpatricks such a fright that they would see the error of their ways. She also needed to send a message to all of the other kids on the estate. She needed to let them know that there was always a way to stand up to bullies.

She lay in bed that night reading her book. After a while, she put it down and lay with one hand behind her head. With the other hand, she stroked her chin. She had thought of the perfect plan. It was a wonderfully wicked plan. That night, she drifted off to sleep with a delicious smile on her face.

During the next day, Harry went to Sam and reminded her that she had carved her name on the back of the game. Sam told Harry that she hadn't. Harry winked at her and said, "Oh, I think you did."

Sam was a little bit slow, but eventually she said, "Oh, yes, now that you mention it, I think that you are right. I did put my name on the back of it."

This was the first step in Harry's wonderfully wicked plan. For her plan to work, Harry needed to gain the trust of the Fitzpatricks. She spent some time hanging around them, but they showed little sign of befriending her. One day, she was sitting on the fence watching them play football, when their ball went over the fence into a garden. The boys were arguing about who should climb over the fence to retrieve it. The problem was that there was a huge and ferocious dog in that garden and the boys were obviously afraid of it. Harry saw her chance. She told the boys that she would climb over the fence and get their ball back for them. They were clearly impressed.

Harry was brave, but even she had butterflies in her stomach as she began to climb the fence. The dog barked the most frightening bark, but Harry held her nerve. When she looked over the fence, she could see that the dog was dripping saliva and pulling on his chain. The ball rested tantalisingly close to the dog, but she thought that she might just be able to reach the ball without getting her hand bitten. She couldn't be absolutely certain of this, though. She also had to worry about the people in the house. If they came out to see why the dog was barking, she would be in deep trouble.

Harry lowered herself into the garden and almost crawled towards the ball. She thought that it was perhaps better for her to leave it, because the dog looked as though it might break its chain and attack her. But, she was made of strong stuff. She held her nerve. She moved slowly towards the ball and quickly threw it back over the fence. She then clambered over the fence again as quickly as she could.

The Fitzpatrick boys gave her a round of applause. They looked upon her in a different light now. All of a sudden, they had a new found respect for her. From that moment on, they started being friendly towards her. This was crucial to her plan. She began spending more time with them. She wasn't a great fan of some of the things they did, but she found that they weren't that bad after all.

She still needed to get even with them, though. Just because she was getting friendly with them didn't mean she could go soft.

Harry became so friendly with the Fitzpatrick boys that she began to go to their flat from time to time. It was another world. The younger children used the older boys for furniture. The pecking order was clear. The older boys lay on the settee and the younger ones balanced on top of them. If you wanted to walk across the living room, you had to pick your way over children lying on the floor or playing with cars.

Bedtime was a very strange scene indeed. The children piled into beds like jelly babies in a bag. It must have been a strange experience to wake up with somebody's toe stuck up your nose.

One day when Harry was at their flat she was asked to stay for something to eat. This called for more bravery than walking into the den of the wild dog. Watching the Fitzpatricks eat was a bit like watching wild pigs fight to the death over a piece of bread. There were noises that sounded a bit like chomping and drooling, but there was also a low murmur of a growl. It was very unusual indeed. Harry thought that cooking tea for her mum, who lay on the settee all day, seemed very normal in comparison to this.

The boys' father put a cake into the middle of the table. He raised his hand to call for silence and slowly whispered a threat to them. He told them that they would pay with their lives if the cake was so much as touched before he gave it out. Harry could tell they believed him. After all, he was pointing a large, broad, bread knife at them as he said it.

Their father turned around slowly to continue his work at the stove. The boys looked at each other, and at the cake, as though they were gun-fighting cowboys waiting for someone to make the first move. As their father left the room, one of the older boys picked up a couple of crumbs that had fallen from the edge of the cake. One of his younger brothers screamed out, "Daddy! Daddy! It's Kevin. He's after stealing the cake."

A thunderous roar could be heard returning to the kitchen. The older boy saw red and slapped his brother around the ear. Their father walked in and seeing what was going on slapped Kevin across the back of his head. The lad was outraged and so picked up the cake and splashed it into his father's face. The table got overturned and a huge food fight started. One of the girls got a bowl of custard over her head and one of the other boys got a crab paste sandwich stuffed in his mouth. People were ducking and diving and bobbing and weaving. Chairs were flying, and assorted food was being splashed up against the wall.

Harry couldn't believe what she was witnessing. She sat in the corner, open mouthed and amazed at what was going on. A toddler was watching from a safe distance in her high chair. She thought it was all very funny indeed, so funny, in fact, that she decided to join in and she poured her own baby food over her head and rubbed it in her hair. And all around her face and sat there laughing.

After a while they noticed the baby was sat there laughing and one of the children joined her. Then another started laughing and then the father joined in. Soon they were all laughing. They started putting their arms around each other and hugging. Harry thought that she must have wandered into a parallel universe. Everybody started scraping food off themselves and their clothes and they slowly drifted into the living room to watch television. Mr Fitzpatrick opened a bottle of beer from his supply down by the side of his chair. He used the bottle opener that always hung from his belt.

A calm fell over them all, which was only broken by the odd chuckle from the father as he reflected upon the whole episode. Perhaps the strangest thing was that nobody spoke of it. They didn't make the slightest effort to clean it up. They didn't even lift the baby out of the high chair. Harry pinched herself to make sure that she wasn't living in some kind of surreal dream. But it was definitely for real. She was a guest in the weird and wonderful world of family life in the high rise.

This calm did give Harry the opportunity to put the next part of her plan into operation. She sneaked off into the bedroom to search for

Sam's stolen game. First, she looked under the beds. She thought to herself that this in itself deserved another bravery award. Most children have the odd smelly sock under their beds but these bedrooms were outrageous. Each bed had the equivalent of a landfill site under it.

Harriet put her head under the first bed, and the smell made her lose her breath. She went cross-eyed and her face went a kind of purple and green colour. She held her throat and tried to suck some life back into her lungs as she fell backwards onto the floor gasping for air.

She recovered and pulled a monster face as she summoned up all her courage to re-enter what she thought must be the stickiest and smelliest place in the world. She fished out a variety of smelly under garments and tossed them to one side or over her shoulder. One garment didn't quite make it and landed on her shoulder. It was a stiff sock with some very nasty stains on it. Harry was struck rigid. She couldn't move this thing off her. Eventually she wriggled free of it and kicked it away from her. This quest was the hardest thing that Harry had ever done in her life. She took a deep breath and carried on with her work. Some of the things that she removed from under those beds were most unpleasant indeed. However, her efforts proved worthwhile. Eventually, she found the stolen game buried under a half eaten pizza. It had a catapult wrapped around it.

Harry put her ear up against the bedroom door. If she worked quickly, she could carve Sam's initials on the back of the game and replace it before she got caught. If anybody noticed she was missing, and came looking for her, she would be in serious trouble. It would be very difficult to make up an excuse for being in the boys' room by herself.

Let's face it, she thought to herself, you would need a really good reason for sneaking into this room.

When Harry didn't clean her flat, it looked like a bombsite, but, even at its worst, it was like a palace compared to this. She half expected a small furry creature to come crawling out looking for clean air.

Harry kept listening out for the Fitzpatrick children as she finished off Sam's initials. She replaced the game where she had found it, and casually made her way back into the living room.

Nobody had missed her. This was great. Her plan was working. After a while, she made her excuses and walked back to her own flat. Harry entered the flat and called out to her mum. There was no answer, so Harry went to check on her. She was fast asleep with a half finished bottle of sherry by her side. Harry smiled. It was nice to be back to sanity again. The tranquil calm of her flat was warm and homely. She was glad to be home.

The next day Harry went to call for Sam. She gave Sam a detailed description of the way she had carved Sam's initials on the back of the game. Harry's plan was to call the police and tell them that the stolen game was in the Fitzpatrick's flat. Sam was well prepared to identify her property when the police found it.

The plan worked a treat. She called the police station and gave them an anonymous tip off. The police retrieved the game and returned it to its rightful owner. The Fitzpatrick boys were given an official warning by the police and told to mend their ways.

Soon, everybody on the estate found out what had happened, and they knew that they could all stand up to the Fitzpatrick family. Sam got her game back and, she also gained confidence from the situation. Sam and Harry became good friends and because of this the Fitzpatricks stopped calling her names.

Harry lay in bed and stroked her chin. She loved it when she got even by using one of her wonderfully wicked plans. She felt particularly content as she drifted off to sleep that night.

Chapter Four

Harry had never been in a school team before. In fact, the only teams they had in their school were for year six children, but the PE teacher wanted to start up some teams for younger children. Harry and her friends thought that this was a great idea and decided to try out for the netball team.

The PE teacher told all of the girls that, if they wanted to be in the team, they would have to come to a practice each week. Quite a few of them agreed. The practice sessions were hard work. It wasn't just netball at the sessions. The girls were asked to do lots of running and exercises as well. Harry loved it. She knew that some of the other girls were better than her at netball, but she thought that she was still in with a chance of making the team. She decided to work as hard as she could to try and get selected and, that way, even if she weren't picked, at least she would know that she had done her best.

Harry had become good friends with a girl in her class called Nicola. Nicola was in a similar position to Harry. There were some better players than her, but, with a lot of hard work, she also thought that she might be able to persuade the teacher that she was worth a place on the team. Both girls worked hard week after week until, eventually, the day came for the team to be announced. It was an exciting time for all of them. Most of them had never played for a team before, so those who were selected were bound to be thrilled and those who were not selected were bound to be hugely disappointed.

It was good news for both Harry and Nicola. They were both selected. They gave each other a big hug. All of the girls who were selected were kind and thoughtful to the girls who had been left out. The girls who hadn't been chosen were taking it very well, and although they were upset, they still congratulated those who were successful. There was one exception. A girl called Mary wasn't as nice as the other girls. She said that Nicola didn't deserve a place in the team and that she only got in because she was the teacher's pet. Everybody, apart from Mary, thought that this was ridiculous and they told Nicola not to take any notice.

Harry was so excited, she felt as though she was skipping on air as she ran home to give her mum the good news. Harry raced upstairs and into the flat. She called out to her mum to tell her what had happened. "Guess what mum? Guess what? I've been selected for the school team to play netball." Her mum was dozing on the settee.

"That's nice dear. Do you want chips for your tea? I've left the money on the side," she replied sleepily.

Harriet was really upset by her mum. "That's nice! Is that all you can say? I'm really proud of what I've done and you can't even be bothered."

Her mum shouted at her and Harry shouted back. A really big argument started and, in the end, Harry picked up the money on the side and said she was going to get her own chips and her mum could starve for all she cared. Harry slammed the door and raced off. Her mum called after her, but it was no use. Harry just ignored her and ran off in the direction of the chip shop.

Harry arrived back home really late. When she came in, well after dark, her mum was all lovey-dovey towards her. She said how sorry she was and Harry said it was all right, really. Deep down, though, she was still upset. Harry's mum tried to get her to talk about it, but Harry said it was no big deal, really. It was just a school team. Harry's mum made them both a nice cup of tea. Harry said that she should run off more often, and they both laughed.

Nicola was still excited about being picked for the netball team the next day. She couldn't stop talking about it. Well, none of them could, really. Nicola said that her mum had bought her a cake and that her Nan had come over with 50p for her. Harry said that it had been a similar kind of thing at her house.

It was a good time to be at school. The lessons were interesting. They did lots of art; painting in particular. They also did lots of music and drama, and they had brilliant PE lessons.

One day though, Nicola's world stood still. She was being a bit naughty. She was wetting paper towels, mashing them up and throwing them at the ceiling in the toilets. There had been a craze for doing it over the last few days. Nicola's problems started when one of the teachers walked into the toilets and caught her red-handed.

Nicola was marched down to the Head Teacher's office. This was serious. The Head started by putting Nicola's name in the 'naughty book'. You had to have done something quite serious just to be put in there. Then she said she wasn't going to talk to Nicola about it until her parents came into school. When her parents did arrive, they were angry and disappointed. Nicola had never really been in trouble before. Her punishment was severe. The Head Teacher said that if Nicola were reported to her for anything at all during the rest of the term, she would not be allowed to play netball for the school.

It was horrible to have something like this hanging over her, but it could have been worse. All she had to do was stay out of trouble. That wouldn't be too hard. After all, she'd never been in serious trouble before.

Nicola was determined not to get into any trouble. She made sure that she did everything that she was supposed to do. She made sure that she didn't put a foot out of line.

Everything was going well. The team was getting better all the time, but Nicola was suddenly called before the Head Teacher again. This time, the Head said that she had been reliably informed that Nicola had been up to her old tricks again. Nicola protested that she hadn't been up to anything at all, but the Head was having none of it.

Someone had been writing on the walls in the girls' toilets and the Head had been told that it was Nicola who was responsible. Nicola said that she had absolutely nothing to do with it, but the Head refused to believe her. She said that Nicola's punishment was to miss out on the big match. Nicola begged, but the Head had made up her mind.

Nicola was distraught. Her parents came up to the school again to try to persuade the Head to change her mind. They told her how excited Nicola had been and that she would not have done anything to risk her place on the team. It made no difference. The Head Teacher had made up her mind and there was no shifting her.

The PE teacher was unhappy. The last thing she wanted to do was to change the team around. Especially when they were working so well together, and there was only one week to go until the big match. The PE teacher also tried to change the Head's mind, but there was to be no change.

Everybody was upset. Everybody except Mary, that was. She was the girl who had said that she thought Nicola had not deserved her selection in the first place. This turn of fate meant that Mary was now in the team in Nicola's place.

Harry and Nicola strongly suspected that Mary was at the bottom of all of this. They suspected that Mary had written on the walls herself and then told the Head Teacher that it was Nicola in order to get Nicola removed from the team and to leave a space open for herself.

Nicola kept bursting into tears all the time. Harry, though, was made of sterner stuff. Instead of getting upset, Harry resolved to think up a wonderfully wicked plan in order to get even with Mary.

That night, Harry lay on her bed hoping for some inspiration. She thought and thought of ways to get even, but no ideas came into her mind. She was determined to get Nicola her place back on the team. She hated it when nasty people got their way over good people.

Night went and morning came, but still no plan emerged in Harry's brain. Harry was becoming quite frustrated, because the match was now only six days away. She had to think of something quite quickly otherwise the smug Miss Mary would get her own way. She had crossed Harriet the Horrible, and nobody did that and got away with it.

By the time Harry went to bed that night, she was still trying to think of a way to get even with Mary. Harry made up her mind that Nicola was going to play for the school team no matter what the cost. That night, she came up with a plan. It was neither wonderful nor wicked, but it was the only one she could think of, so she decided to use it.

The next day, Harry went to see her Head Teacher. She told the Head that she was feeling guilty and remorseful. She confessed to writing on the wall. The Head Teacher was taken aback. She flew into quite a rage. She shouted about how cruel Harriet had been to let her friend take all the blame. She told Harriet that she was a spiteful, cruel child who only cared about herself. She said that she was a shameless, selfish little girl who should be ashamed.

Nicola was reinstated in the school team and now it was Harry's turn to be left out. Nicola knew what Harry had done for her and she was very grateful. Harry told Nicola that this was not the end, though. They both knew that it was Mary who was the guilty party, and so Nicola and Harry made a pact that they would one day prove that it was Mary who had written on the wall.

The PE teacher didn't think badly of Harry and asked her to continue training with the team. Harry promised that she would. She promised that she would go and watch them play and cheer them on all the way.

There were only five days to go until the big match, and the girls practised each and every lunchtime in the school playground. Harry was enjoying the practice, despite the knowledge that she couldn't play in the match, when she heard her name being called in the distance. She had a sinking feeling. She knew that call. It was her mother's voice, and it had an unhappy urgency about it.

"Harry! Harry! Come on! We've got to go – right now!"

Harry argued with her mum saying that she couldn't go because of the big match. She couldn't possibly miss it. Harry's mum said that they had to go straight away and that was that.

Harry hugged Nicola and said that she was sorry, but she had to go. Nicola couldn't believe it. Harry told her mum that before they left, she had something very important to say to the Head Teacher. Harry's mum said that they didn't have a minute to spare and she dragged Harry away. All that she was carrying this time was one black bin liner full of clothes. Harry's mum was looking nervously all around her. She told Harry to keep her voice down and to be quiet.

Harry tried shouting, "Good luck for the match!" to Nicola but her mum pulled her away and told her again to be quiet.

Chapter Five

Harry's mum held her close. She walked to the end of the school building and pressed her back against the wall. She edged her way to the end and peered round the corner. When she was sure the coast was clear, she dragged Harry by the arm and raced across the road into a sweet shop.

Harry had seen her mum in an agitated state before, but this was by far the worst she had ever been. She pulled Harry in behind the counter and made her crouch down. She looked out of the window to make sure that they weren't being followed. The man who owned the sweet shop couldn't believe his eyes.

"What is this you are doing in my shop?" He was waving his arms around and shrugging his shoulders.

Harry's mum knocked over some sweets by accident.

"Hey!" the man yelled. "You'll have to pay for them."

"Oh! Go and boil your head!" Harry's mum shouted back. Then she looked at Harry and started laughing. So Harry started laughing too.

Harry's mum stood up and gave the sweet shop owner a piece of her mind. She pulled his hat down over his eyes. She picked up a jar of sherbet and threw it over him. He couldn't see and put his hands out in front of him to try and catch Harry's mum, but he was just grabbing thin air. He couldn't stop himself from sneezing.

"Ahh!" he said, as he tried to catch his breath, "Ahh! Ahh!"

His customers stood back from him.

"Ahh Choo!!!" and he sneezed all over his customers. An old lady hit him over the head with her umbrella, and a small child kicked him in the shin.

"Ooooh! Eeeeeee! Owwwww!" he cried out and fell back in a heap. Harry and her mum couldn't stop laughing as they ran through the shop towards the back where the owner lived. They made their way through the back door, out into a side street and ran off down the road.

Harry's mum seemed to have lightened up a bit, but she was still looking over her shoulder to make sure they weren't being followed. She became very serious again when she looked over her shoulder one time. She yanked hold of Harry and dragged her into the nearest shop. It was a clothes shop. Harry's mum bundled her black bin liner under the counter and told Harry to hide under some clothes. Harry stood behind a rack of dresses. She was well hidden except for the bottom of her legs and her feet that were sticking out. Harry's mum picked up a wig from a dummy and she put that on, along with a hat that she had found on a shelf. She put on an overall, and quickly started dusting the shelves at the back of the shop.

It seemed like ages that Harry was forced to stand still while her mum busied herself in disguise at the back of the shop. The staff stood motionless. They had never seen anything like it. Harry's mum begged them to carry on as normal, and, to their credit, they tried their best to act as though nothing unusual was happening.

After a while, a customer came in and started browsing around. All was fine until she lifted up the dress that Harry was hiding behind.

Harry gave a little squeal and the customer jumped in the air.

"Ahhh!" she screamed. "This dress! It's alive!"

Harry raised the arm of the dress and the customer gave another scream.

"Ahhh!" she screamed. "It's alive! It's alive! And it's coming after me! Ahhh! Help! Help!"

She ran off out of the shop, screaming murder. All the passers-by started looking into the shop to see what it was that had startled her.

Harry's mum told Harry that she had been very discreet and that she was proud of her. She shouted a "thank you" to the staff and asked them where the back door was. She grabbed the bin liner and ran off out of the shop.

Once they were out in the back, they found that there was no gate for their escape. There was nothing else for it. They dragged a bin up against the fence. Harry's mum hitched up her skirt and tucked it into her knickers. She threw the bin liner over the fence, and the two of them climbed over. As soon as they were both over, they raced off down the road as fast as they could. There were two people getting into a taxi, and Harry's mum asked them if they could share. The people asked her where she was going, but Harry's mum just said, "Wherever you're going!"

They said they were going to the coach station.

"Brilliant!" said Harry's mum.

And, with that, Harry and her mum jumped into the back of the cab.

When they got to their destination, Harry's mum said, "Now, you must let me pay for this. I insist!" But the people said that it was all right and that she didn't need to pay.

"OK!" said Harry's mum cheerfully, and she shouted goodbye as she rushed out of the cab. They ran towards a coach that was just leaving and jumped aboard. She asked if it was a long distance coach and the driver replied that it was only local. He said that all of the "out of town" coaches were at the back of the station. Harry's mum explained to the driver that they couldn't get back off the front of the coach so they were going to sneak off through the emergency exit at the back. She told him not to say a word, if anybody asked about them. Before the driver could register a complaint, they made their way to the back of the coach, nodding to the passengers as they passed by.

They gingerly sneaked off the coach, and bent down to tiptoe through the local coaches until they came to a long distance one.

"This'll do!" Harry's mum said, and they climbed on board.

When they had settled down, and the coach had started moving, Harry asked her mum why they were always on the run. She told her that there were just some things that children don't get to know about. She said it was time for

them to move and that was that!

After a couple of hours, they stopped off at a service station. Harry and her mum got something to

48

eat and sat down at a table. A huge red-faced man, with a stomach so large that it was bursting through his shirt, came and sat down beside them. He had horrible greasy skin and something that looked like a little boil on the side of his nose. Harry thought he was disgusting. His hair was all greasy and he'd combed it across his head to hide his bald patch.

Harry's mum and the fat man started chatting away to each other and Harry began to feel trapped, as he started taking up more and more space on her side of the table. After a while, they found out his name was Derek.

I might have known, thought Harry to herself, he looks like a Derek. Out loud, Harry said, "It doesn't work, you know." The two adults looked at her and asked her what didn't work. "Combing your hair across your bald patch. It doesn't work. Everybody knows you're bald, you know," she replied boldly.

The two adults looked embarrassed. Harry's mum gave a look of vicious disapproval. Harry wanted to go to the toilet and the man had to move his legs to one side to let her through. Harry had to squeeze past him.

When she finally managed to prise herself out, she turned to give him a nasty look and dusted herself down. Harry's mum gave a false smile to the fat man and said, "I don't know where she gets it from," and then she turned to look at her daughter with a savage grimace on her face.

Harry took her time. She wandered around the services for a while so that she wouldn't have to spend any more time next to Derek than she absolutely had to. When she returned, she found the two of them holding hands and giggling.

"Oh no, mum! You can't be serious."

"Don't be silly, Harry." Harry's mum gave another of her false smiles to Derek. "I want you to be nice to Derek. He's offered us a lift to his home town, where he lives in a big house all by himself."

Harry couldn't believe it. She told her mum that they needed to talk.

"Later, dear," her mum replied, squeezing her hand and shooting one of her sickly smiles towards Derek, "this isn't quite the time or place."

Harry knew it was hopeless. They always ended up doing exactly what her mum wanted. The car journey was awful, right from the beginning. Her mum said how gorgeous the car was and started giggling. She giggled all the way down the motorway. She laughed at everything Derek said, even though it wasn't remotely funny. She kept touching his hand and holding onto his arm. From time to time, she would burst out laughing and rest her head on his shoulder. Harry thought that any more of this would make her sick.

By the time they got to Derek's house, her mum had told him that they had nowhere to stay and he had offered to put them up for a while. Harry was turning into Harriet the Horrible by the second. When they got to the house, it was disgusting. Her mother would be quite at home with this man. It was the worst mess Harry had ever seen. Derek said it was the maid's day off, and Harry's mother fell into fits of laughter. Harry wanted to scream.

Derek had a dog. The dog had obviously been left in the house for some time because there was dog pooh all over the hall floor. To

Harry's amazement, Derek ignored it and immediately went to pour himself and Harry's mum a drink instead. They giggled away for about half an hour until, eventually, Derek said that he would go and clear up the mess because it wasn't very inviting. Harry's mum told him not to. They were there now and they would pull their weight. With that, she shouted out to Harry to be a good girl and clear up the dog mess in the hall.

Harry was so amazed she couldn't speak. She couldn't even breathe. She stood in the hallway gasping for breath. Her mum looked up and saw her standing gulping for air. Her mum nodded at her with the side of her head. Harry was in shock. This took the biscuit even by her mum's standards. Harry's mum made it clear that she wanted Harry to do it without any argument.

Harry's mum rubbed salt into her wounds by then telling her to take the dog for a walk. Harry thought that it was a horrible mutt. It was a big fat boxer dog with a skin complaint. The dog dragged Harry around for about half an hour before returning her home. Harry put her prettiest voice on and asked her mum if she could talk to her. She told her mum that she hated everything; she hated the place, she hated the dog and, most of all, she hated Derek.

"He's big and fat and ugly. He's got a skin complaint and he smells!" she finished.

Her mum agreed, but said that he was being kind enough to put them up.

Harry said, "I was talking about the dog!"

They both laughed and Harry's mum promised that it wouldn't be forever.

No, Harry thought to herself, nothing ever is.

Harry made cheese and beans on toast for herself. As the only food in the house was cheese, beans and bread, it was all she could do really. It was a mistake, though, because Derek asked if she could do him some as well. Her mum piped up and asked for some too. That was all Harry needed. Now she had two adults to wait on. Cheese and beans on toast were an instantaneous success. Derek asked for it the next day and the day after and the day after that.

Harry had become quite unhappy. She didn't really like her new school. Her new teacher liked to shout a lot. Harry was determined to pull him down a peg or two, but first she had a more pressing engagement. She had to find a way of prising her mum away from the cheesy grease ball.

She lay in bed at night with one hand behind her head and the other stroking her chin. She had to think of a wonderfully wicked plan. Night after night, she lay there hoping for a good idea until, eventually, it came to her. She couldn't think of a way to get her mum to want to leave Derek, but surely she could come up with a way of making Derek want to get rid of her mum.

The next day, Harry waited for her mum to leave the house, and then she started to put her wonderfully wicked plan into operation. She made Derek his favourite cheese and beans on toast. She made him a nice hot cup of tea and she sat down beside him. She asked him if he really liked her mum. He said that he did. In fact, he said that she was the best thing that had happened to him in years. Harry said that she was pleased. She said that she liked his house and then she asked him if half of it belonged to her mum now that they were all living there together. Derek stopped eating. He said it most definitely did not. It was his house and nobody else's. Not now, not ever. Harry told him that she understood. She asked him if he would have to pay her mum lots of money if he wanted her to leave. Derek said of course he wouldn't. Harry asked if that only happened when someone stayed in your house for a long time.

Derek began to be alarmed. Harry continued, "Oh, by the way. Have you found out about her little problem yet?" Derek said that he hadn't and asked what the problem was. Harry said that it was nothing really, but she told him to keep his valuables safe.

"What?" he said. "Is she going to steal all of my things?"

Derek started pacing up and down the front room and Harry retreated to her bedroom.

When Harry's mum came home, she was full of smiles. She

danced her way over to Derek and pinched his cheek, but Derek pulled away.

"What's wrong?" she asked.

Derek said that he had been doing some thinking. He said that it was time that Harry's mum and Harry found somewhere else to live. And he said that, if they were thinking of helping themselves to his possessions, he had them all marked and the police would be able to trace them and they'd throw her into prison.

Harry's mum was shocked. She started to hurl insults at him, his house, his dog and his possessions. She said that she and her daughter weren't staying a minute longer where they obviously weren't wanted. She went to Harry's room to tell her it was time to leave. If she was surprised to see Harry waiting for her with her clothes already packed in a black plastic bag, she didn't show it.

The two of them left and, as Harry was going out of the door, she waved to Derek and blew him a little kiss. She loved it when one of her wonderfully wicked plans proved to be successful.

Harry and her mum found a hostel to stay in. It could only be temporary, but obviously that wasn't a problem. Her next problem was to sort out her new teacher.

It shouldn't be hard, Harry thought to herself; after all, I'm something of an expert now.

Chapter Six

"Stand up, boy!" or "Stop that at once, you nasty little girl."

There was always some reason for Mr Wright to shout. All the children had, inevitably, christened Mr Wright Mr Wrong as soon as he had arrived at the school.

He took to shouting at Harry. He was, quite possibly, the most obnoxious teacher that Harry had ever come across. He had yellow, stained fingers and a stooped back. He was one of those teachers who had a habit of looking over his glasses. He was quite old and skinny and he never shaved properly. His elbows had patches on them, and his clothes were old and baggy. Right, thought Harry. We'll soon sort you out!

Harry lay in bed stroking her chin. She wanted to think up one of her wonderfully wicked plans, but she didn't want to rush into the first idea that came into her mind. She wanted to make sure that she got good and even and she wanted to make sure that she had lots of fun as well. Eventually, after a lot of thought, she came up with a good idea, and it made her smile one of her wicked smiles. She went to sleep happy that night.

Harry bided her time until old Wrighty was at his worst. He was humiliating a boy in the class who had done badly in a spelling test.

"You're a stupid little boy! Stupid! Stupid! Stupid! What are you?" he poked the boy in the chest each time he said the word "stupid".

The boy agreed that he was stupid and started to cry. Harry's eyes half closed and she went into "Horrible" mode.

At playtime, she went to talk to the boy in the playground. She asked him if he wanted to get even with old Wrighty, and, of course, he did. She told the boy of her plan. He agreed that, from that moment on, he would go on strike. Any time the teacher asked him to do anything, he was to say that he couldn't do it. No matter how many times Mr Wright explained something, he just had to say that he was sorry, but he just didn't understand it.

As part of the plan, Harry, too, was saying that she couldn't understand things. Even the most simple of things she pretended were too hard for her. Old Wrighty asked her to write a book review. Harry asked him what she had to write. He told her to write what she thought of the book.

"But, I don't think anything about it, Sir," Harry said, in her most sincere and angelic voice. Old Wrighty asked her if it was a good book. She said that she didn't know. He began to get agitated.

"Surely you must know whether it was a good book or not."

"No, Sir," Harry said, in a pathetic little voice.

"Well, was it funny or sad?" Wrighty tried again.

"I don't know, Sir," Harry answered.

He was getting angry, "Well, can you at least write down what the book was about, then?"

"I can't remember, Sir!" Harry was enjoying this now.

Old Wrighty started to gnash his teeth together.

"Oh! Oh! Just do something else, then. Read a book or draw a picture or something!"

"Yes, Sir!" Harry replied eagerly.

This was too easy. Harry was winning already. Old Wrighty went over to the boy and told him to do some two times tables questions. He could have done them easily, but he said that he was sorry, but he couldn't do them. Mr Wright told him that of course he could; he had done them lots of times before.

"I'm sorry, Sir. I can't do them." The boy sat there staring blankly at the teacher.

Wrighty started waving his hands about. He took a handkerchief from his pocket and wiped his brow.

"Now look here," he pointed his bony finger at the child. "You can do these sums and I want you to do them now! Without any messing about! Do you hear me?!!!"

"I'm not messing about, Sir. I can't do them. I just can't do them," the boy answered calmly.

"Oh! Oh! Oh! Just do some colouring in or something!" Mr Wright shouted in exasperation. "But, do it quietly!"

At playtime, Harry told the other children about the plan. She said that, if everyone did the same, old Mr Wrong would have a fit. The other children thought that it was a brilliant idea. None of them liked their teacher. They were all really pleased at the idea of seeing him get his comeuppance.

Back in the class, Mr Wright got out some textbooks and told the class to copy a map from the book. One by one, the children raised their hands and said that they were finding it too hard. To each one, old Wright said, "Of course you can! Of course you can! You've done this before! You can do that. It's easy." His face was getting redder by the minute. His veins were sticking out of his head and his neck. His eyes were bulging. "Do your work! Do your work!" he was screaming.

All over the class, the children were saying, "We can't do it! It's too hard! Can you help us, Sir?"

"No! No! No! I can't help you all. Just do your work! Do your work!" He was jumping up and down and foaming at the mouth. He started striding around the class like a demented robot.

"I can't cope! I can't cope!" he was shouting. "Help! Help! Somebody call for the Head Teacher! Help! Help! I can't cope. Somebody help me."

Old Wrighty lay down on the floor, having a fit. He was making strange baaing sounds, like a troubled sheep, with his legs kicking out from time to time in an involuntary flick. He was muttering under his breath. "Help me. Help. I've never seen anything like it. They can all do the work. I know they can. I've seen them. I know they can do it, they can, they can. They're on strike. That's what's happening. They're on strike. It's a mutiny. There's a mutiny in my classroom! Help! Somebody help me. I can't cope. I can't cope."

Somebody had gone for the Head Teacher. When she arrived at the classroom, she couldn't believe what she saw. Old Wrighty was flat out on his back, making strange noises. The Head Teacher called for the caretaker and they carried Mr Wright out on a stretcher. He was muttering nonsense under his breath. "It wasn't my fault. They all stood together. They wouldn't do as they were told."

As they carried him out of the room, he called back to the children, "You horrors, I'll be back! I'll be back one day! I'm not beaten yet!"

When the teachers were well out of earshot, all of the children cheered. They picked Harry up on their shoulders and sang,

"*For she's a jolly good fellow,*
For she's a jolly good fellow,
For she's a jolly good fellow,
And so say all of us!"

Children clapped their hands, sang songs and danced on the tables and chairs. "Hooray!" they shouted. "Hooray! We've finally got rid of old Wrighty! Hip! Hip! Hooray!"

Before long, the school bell went and it was home time. The Head Teacher came into the room and tried to make the children become quiet.

"Oh dear me!" she said. "This is most irregular. Mr Wright is one of our finest teachers. He really is. I don't know what to say. I suppose you had all better have the rest of the week off as there's nobody left to teach you."

All the children cheered and shouted louder than ever. They all ran out of school as fast as they could. They jostled past the Head who was bounced this way and that as the children left. "Oh dear!" she muttered under her breath. "Oh dear! This is most irregular. What will poor Mrs Wright have to say? Who on earth can I get to teach the class now? Nobody will dare to come in here after this. Oh dear, dear me. This is most irregular, most irregular indeed!" She shuffled off down the corridor in a rather confused daze, muttering to herself as she went.

Chapter Seven

It was great news in the classroom. When they eventually found a teacher who was brave enough to take the class, she found that the children were not so bad after all. They were quite hard working and they tried their best to do work that was a bit hard for them as well. All they needed was a teacher who was nice to them.

Poor old Wrighty, thought Harry, he just had to find out the hard way, that was all.

Harry's mum had not been idle. She had been doing her usual work of finding somewhere to live. When Harry got home from school, her mum gave her the good news. She had found somewhere nice to live. She warned Harry that it was only temporary. No surprise there, thought Harry. Everything is temporary in our lives.

Harry's mum took her to their new temporary home. Two men had offered to put them up for a while. They had a beautiful house. The garden was like one that you would see in a painting, and the inside of the house was even more beautiful. All of the furniture was highly polished. You could see your reflection in it. There was a lovely scent in the air from cut flowers that were in almost every room. Patrick and Brian were the kindest men that Harry had ever met. They were always making a fuss of her, right from the first moment they met.

Patrick had a cat called Oscar and Brian had one called Quentin. Patrick said that they were silly cats because they didn't know to whom they belonged. Both cats purred at Patrick and Brian and they were the most pampered cats in the world. If they weren't being stroked as they lay on a cushion, then they were being held and stroked. Patrick and Brian had an endless amount of love and affection. When they weren't smothering the cats with kindness, they were doing things for each other or for Harry and her mum.

It was the first time that Harry could ever remember having all of her washing and ironing done for her. They wouldn't let her do any housework whatsoever. They said that she was a guest and anyway, they said, children should play because they would have plenty of work to do when they were adults.

Harry had never been happier in her life. Her mum had got a job and had bought her some nice clothes. Patrick and Brian were the best adults that she had ever met. Harry had only ever listened to music on the radio, but Patrick and Brian introduced her to classical music; they told her all about it. They played beautiful ballet music and told her the stories behind each ballet.

They could see how much Harry was enjoying it. They couldn't believe that she had never been to see a ballet in her life. For a special surprise they bought tickets to take her to see her very first ballet. It was a big production of Swan Lake. They offered to take Harry's mum as well, but she declined the offer. As part of the surprise, Patrick and Brian went out and bought Harry a new dress. It was the most beautiful dress that Harry had ever seen. She gave them both a huge hug and all three of them had to fight back tears.

Harry loved the ballet. She loved dressing up. She loved the theatre. She loved the music.

She loved the dancing. She loved the occasion. She loved being with Patrick and Brian. They made her feel like a princess.

Harry lay in bed that night and had a quiet little cry to herself. She was happier than she had ever been, and she didn't want anything to change. She knew it was only temporary and that made her sad. She wanted everything to stay as it was forever. She wondered if she would be allowed to stay with Patrick and Brian when her mum next said that it was time for them to hit the road. She hated herself for thinking it. She loved her mum really. She just couldn't help herself from feeling so safe and secure and settled with Patrick and Brian. She decided to put all thoughts of moving out of her mind. She decided that she wouldn't think of leaving until she absolutely had to.

School was becoming really good. Her new teacher was in charge of the school play. It was great, because Harry had been given a really good part. On the day she was chosen, she raced all the way home to tell Patrick and Brian her good news. They were thrilled for her. They decided to have a celebration. Patrick made one of his delicious lasagnes and a lovely fresh fruit salad for their evening meal, and Brian opened some of his best home made wine. They even let Harry have a sip that was mixed with orange juice.

In the evenings that followed, Patrick and Brian read through Harry's words with her. They took the part of the other actors and helped her learn her lines. It was the best fun that she had ever had in her life. She loved playing with Patrick and Brian, especially when they let her help with the cooking. They taught her how to cook more adventurous meals. It was just the best time.

One day, Harry's idyll was, as ever, shattered. Her mum woke her up early and told her to come downstairs quickly. She knew the signs. Patrick and Brian were both standing downstairs waiting for her. They were stern faced and sombre. Harry's mum hugged them both and thanked them for being such good friends. Harry hugged them as tight as she could. There were tears in her eyes. This was the moment she had been dreading. Her mum, as usual, had said that it was time to leave. Harry felt sad at the thought of leaving her school and friends. She bit her lip as she thought of missing the school play that she had worked so hard for. All of this meant little, though, compared to the thought of leaving Patrick and Brian. She couldn't even try to fight back her tears. She cried uncontrollably as she flung her arms around them both. She didn't want to go. She wanted to ask her mum if she could stay, but she couldn't make herself say the words. Patrick and Brian weren't saying very much at all. Harry could tell they were as sad about her leaving as she was. They drove Harry and her mum to the train station, and hugged them again before they left. Harry could see that Brian's eyes were all watery and wet. Harry leant out of the door window of the train. She could just see Patrick putting his arm around Brian to comfort him as the train pulled out of the station.

The train journey was long and silent. Harry and her mum stared out of the window. After a while, Harry's mum told her that Patrick and Brian were the first men that she had ever met that had not wanted anything from her.

Chapter Eight

Harriet just didn't want to face a new place to live. She just didn't want to face a new school. She really wanted to be back with Patrick and Brian. From time to time, she would daydream about the ballet. She could imagine herself being a great ballerina and collecting flowers and applause and running backstage to be greeted by Patrick and Brian who were her two greatest supporters. It wasn't to be. Her time with Patrick and Brian was precious. It was a brief summer idyll in which she felt that she had swapped her life with somebody who was more fortunate than her.

Reality had a habit of being pretty grim for Harriet. She was quite used to the routine of joining a new school. The Head Teachers were all smiles, and said that they hoped she would be happy at their little school. This school was no exception.

Harry's teacher was quite unusual. She was twice the size of most teachers. She had a great big posh hairdo. She always looked as though she had just walked out of the hairdresser's shop. She had a great pile of make-up caked all over her face. Her lipstick looked like a little girl's who had been playing dressing up. It was squashed all over her mouth. She wore high heels and her skirt was far too tight for her huge bottom to fit into. Her skirt was so tight that she couldn't put each foot forward more than a few centimetres when she walked. This meant that she shuffled along like a Japanese woman in traditional dress.

Like all teachers when you first meet them, Mrs Camalot had a big smile. Hers was bigger than most, because she had such a huge mouth that took up half her face. She spoke very nicely and was very polite to Harriet. Harry was too wise to be taken in, though. She knew that teachers showed their real colours once the classroom door was closed and there were no other adults around. As nice as Mrs Camalot seemed, Harry decided that she would reserve judgement until she had seen her in the classroom for a few days.

Mrs Camalot asked one of the girls to show Harriet around the school and to stay with her during the day to show her the school

didn't like to say, but she knew
_d pick up school routines faster
_ildren. After all, she had more
exp_ _an most.

Mrs Camalot turned out to be quite
average, as teachers go. Harry had known better
teachers, but in fairness to her, she had known
worse teachers as well. The peculiar thing about
Mrs Camalot was that she used to scoff food all
of the time. She brought in a big bag of goodies
in the morning, and she gradually ate her way
through them during the day. She told the
children she had a tummy problem that meant
she had to nibble food from time to time. Harry
thought her real problem was that her tummy
was so big she had to keep scoffing food all day
to keep it topped up.

Every day was the same routine for Mrs
Camalot. She started with a chocolate bar or two
during registration. Then, about half an hour
later, she would eat a couple of bananas. At
break time, she would eat cream crackers
sandwiched around a pound block of cheese.
She drank tea out of a huge mug that was more
like a small bucket. Harry thought that Mrs

Camalot probably ate the equivalent of a baby pig every day. It made Harry sick just to think of it. After her sandwiches at lunchtime, she always ate a massive slice of cake that usually had double thick chocolate or fresh cream in it. Although her name was Mrs Camalot, the children called her Mrs Eatalot, with good reason.

Gradually, Harry came to dislike Mrs Eatalot. She was really lazy. She just sat in her chair all day giving out her orders. Another thing that Harry didn't like was the way that they never did PE. Every week, when they were getting changed, Mrs Eatalot would say that they were too noisy and she would tell them to get changed back into their school clothes. After that, PE would be cancelled. Harry suspected that they didn't ever do PE because Eatalot didn't want to do it and, as Harry's mum would say, "that was that"!

Each year, Eatalot arranged for her class to visit a chocolate factory. She said that it was a special treat for the children. Harry believed that it was probably an even more special treat for her.

Harry and the other children did look forward to the trip, though, and with good reason because it was a great day out. Everyone had to dress in white overalls. No jewellery was allowed and everybody, even the boys, had to wear a hair net for hygiene reasons.

As well as finding out all about chocolate and its history, where it comes from and how it's made, the children also got to eat lots of the finished product. Everybody ate more chocolate than they would normally eat in a month. Even Eatalot did, and that took some doing.

Whenever a tray of chocolate was put out for the class, Eatalot would be the first to dive in and grab a handful for herself. She ate five times as much as anybody else. Harry looked at her with one of her more sinister looks and thought to herself, you are a great big fat greedy tub of lard, aren't you? Then, she smiled a sweet little smile at Mrs Eatalot, and Eatalot tried to smile a gentle little smile back, but it was hard because she was cramming a handful of chocolates into her mouth at the time.

There was a nice guide who was showing them round and talking to them. Harry thought that the guide had probably seen a lot of people get rather carried away with the free chocolates in her time, but even she pulled some rather peculiar faces when she saw how Eatalot was stuffing her face.

The guide left the teacher and the children to enjoy their free chocolate. Mrs Eatalot crammed more and more into her mouth. When all the chocolates were gone, Mrs Eatalot caught sight of a batch of gooey runny chocolate mix that hadn't set yet. She put her hand in and scooped out some of the thick, sweet mixture and licked it off her hands. She liked it so much that she scooped up more and more. She got so carried away that she plunged her whole arm into the mixture and dragged up as much as she could gather.

When the guide returned, the gooey chocolate was dripping off Eatalot's arm. She was frantically licking it off. The guide stood staring in amazement as Eatalot tried, rather sheepishly, to shake off the dripping chocolate and to pretend it wasn't really there. She looked quite a sight with chocolate all over her face, dripping off her chin and a bucket full of the gooey mixture stuck to her arm. Harry thought that it served her right – the greedy pig.

As they were leaving the factory, the guide gave Mrs Eatalot a big bag of chocolates to share between the children when they got back to school. Harry was given the job of carrying the bag back to school and it was quite a weight. When they arrived back at school, Mrs Eatalot said that she would look after the chocolates overnight so that little hands weren't tempted to steal any of them.

The next morning, Mrs Eatalot brought the chocolates into school and gave them to Harry to hand out to the class. Harry could feel that the bag was seriously depleted. She immediately turned to Mrs Eatalot and asked her where all the chocolates had gone.

"They're all there, dear. That's all there were, I can assure you."

Harry knew that she was lying. At least half of the chocolates had gone and she knew that Eatalot had stolen them and scoffed the lot. That was it. Eatalot had crossed Harriet and that was her one big mistake. It was time for Harriet the Horrible to emerge and sort her out.

That night, Harry took up her customary stance in bed and began to hatch a wonderfully wicked plan. It wasn't hard to think of how to get even with Eatalot. It had to be through her food. Harry quickly came up with a plan. In fact, it was quite a delicious plan and wonderful and wicked – yes, a most delicious plan.

The very next day, Harry began to put her plan into action. She didn't want to show her hand too soon, so she started with some small antics. She went to Eatalot's food supply early one morning and cut a slice off her thick chocolate cake. When Eatalot came to eat it, she looked a little puzzled. Harry could just imagine her saying to herself, surely my piece of cake was bigger than that. I'm sure I cut myself a bigger piece than that. I'm sure I did. Eatalot actually scratched her head as she looked at it.

Harry enjoyed her tease, but that was only the beginning. During the next day, Harry again sneaked into Eatalot's supply bag and this time she relieved her of a handful of her favourite biscuits. It was most amusing for Harry to see Eatalot looking exceedingly puzzled as she moved the contents of her bag around looking for her biscuits. Again, Harry took delight in imagining her thinking that she'd put more biscuits in. Eatalot did look extremely puzzled and more than a little bit upset.

By the next day, it was time for Harry to pick up the pace. This time she left the biscuits and cake alone, but she took a knife and spread a thick layer of mustard over the sandwiches. Eatalot attacked her sandwiches with her usual zeal. From time to time, she stopped and stared at her sandwich as though there was something a little strange about it, but it didn't stop her eating them. She chobbled away some more and pulled a rather strange face as though some odd sensations were taking place in her mouth.

Harry could just imagine her thinking, these sandwiches taste rather peculiar but they're exactly the same as usual - the same thick layers of butter and slabs of ham in between the same bread. Only Harry knew what the strange new sensation was.

After Eatalot had finished her sandwiches, she gave out a little burp and then patted her stomach. "Do excuse me children," she said in her politest voice. And then she patted her stomach again. Just then, the Head Teacher walked into the classroom with a message for Mrs Eatalot. She was just in time to hear Eatalot give out a great belch.

All of the class reacted by saying, "Ugggh! That's horrible!"

"Oh dear!" said Mrs Eatalot, "I'm so sorry, Head Teacher, there must have been something unusual in my lunch today. I can't think what it could be because I made my lunch exactly as I usually do."

The Head Teacher looked at her in a most unforgiving manner and walked out of the room without comment. She clearly wasn't very pleased. It wasn't the done thing to go belching all over the children. As ever, Harry loved it when one of her wonderfully wicked plans came to fruition. But, she had only just begun with this one.

The next day, Harry decided to go for the grand prix of pranks. She took a giant jar of extra hot curry powder to school with her… and rubbed her hands just to think of the fun that she was going to have with it.

When the coast was clear, Harry sneaked under the teacher's desk and went to work on her master plan. She took Eatalot's cake out of her bag. It was perfect. She had brought a huge coffee cake with almonds and chocolate chips. It was filled with a particularly gooey fresh cream and coffee mixture. This was ideal because Harry could put her extra hot curry powder all over the mixture and Eatalot wouldn't notice until she sunk her teeth deep into it. And, by then, it would be too late. Harry dolloped and mixed the entire contents of the jar into the middle of the cake and then she carefully put it back in the bag.

All morning, Harry found it hard to think of anything else. Looking forward to seeing Eatalot slobbering over an extra hot curry cake was worse than waiting for Christmas. By the time Eatalot finally took her cake out of her bag, Harry was on the edge of her seat with excitement. Mrs Eatalot held the cake in front of her and licked her lips. Her eyes grew wide with anticipation. She opened her mouth as wide as she could and took a great huge bite into the cake. She let out a scream at once. "Aggghhh!"

she cried. "My mouth's on fire! Aggghhh! Aggghhh!"

She tried to spit the cake out, but it was so thick that it stuck to the roof of her mouth. She couldn't swallow it and she couldn't get rid of it.

"Help!" she gurgled and spat. "Help!" She tried to say "My mouth's on fire", but it just sounded like "My puffs faf faf!"

All of the children looked at her in amazement. Only Harry knew what was happening.

"My paff haf hath harf!" Eatalot cried as she jumped up and down holding her throat.

Mrs Eatalot took some flowers out of a vase and tried to drink the water, but her mouth was so full of the curried cake that the water just splattered and splashed all over her face. Eatalot was clutching her throat with one hand and the vase with the other. She was doing a Highland fling in front of the class!

The Head Teacher came in to see what all the noise and commotion was about, and all she found was Mrs Eatalot spitting curry cake all over the children. "Well, really!" the Head Teacher said.

"Nof nath muth mithend!" Mrs Eatalot shouted in reply, spraying curry cake all over the Head Teacher as well.

The Head Teacher stood rigid in shock. Eatalot tried to wipe the half eaten curry cake off the Head Teacher but all she did was rub it into her nice clean dress.

There was a big glass of water on the side and Eatalot grabbed it and gulped it down. "Aggghhh! Ugghh!!!" she screamed even louder than before. Harry had poured a whole packet of salt into the water and Eatalot had swallowed the lot.

"Aggghh!!! Uggghhh!! Eeee!!! Agghh!" she started off all over again and again she sprang into her Highland fling.

All of the children laughed and cheered at the dancing teacher in front of them. Suddenly,

Eatalot stood motionless. A giant gurgling sound came from her huge tummy.

"Oh, no!" she screamed. The gurgling and the whirling got louder and much worse. "Oh, heck!" she cried. "Excuse me, Head Teacher," she said, as she hugged her tummy and ran out of the room. "I think I've got to pay a visit – quickly!" she screamed, as she ran out of the room and down the corridor.

The Head Teacher looked down at the messy curry splodge all down her nice new dress. "Er, right, children," she said. "Er, well, I suppose you'd better run along to the playground and have an extra playtime."

"Yesss!!" all of the children cheered and ran out of the class. Harry had a little smile to herself. She stroked her chin as she thought, Hmm! I love it when one of my wonderfully wicked plans works out well. And this one certainly did. I will always remember it as my wonderful and DELICIOUSLY wicked plan.

That day, Harriet went home happily.

Chapter Nine

Harry's mum was the world champion at finding somewhere to stay. She had found a woman who said that they could stay as long as they liked. It was a very sparse flat. There were no carpets, just a couple of settees and a TV in the main room. The woman who lived there had twin boys who were a fair bit younger than Harry. She didn't mind the boys. They were a bit noisy at times, but, she thought to herself, beggars can't be choosers. It was nice of the woman to put them up.

The boys were always talking or shouting. They ran around the flat with toy aeroplanes, making roaring noises as they raised the planes up and down or made them loop the loop. It was quite a big flat. There used to be a man who lived with them, but, when the couple split up, he left with his two children so there was plenty of space. Harry had her own room. It was scarcely big enough for a bed to fit in, but it was her own private space. Harry loved to lie in that bedroom. Sometimes, she would think up wonderfully wicked plans, but most of all she loved to lie down and remember what life was like with Patrick and Brian. She loved to imagine herself back in their beautiful garden with all its lovely smells and colours. She could just see herself back in their living room with Patrick on his hands and knees, while she rode on his back like a horse, with Brian clapping his hands and laughing. They were great days.

Harry's mum had found a soul mate. The woman who had put them up was, in many ways, just like Harry's mum. She liked avoiding housework. She liked ignoring her children. She liked to sit and watch daytime television all day. She liked to drink lager and wine and she liked to go out at night and stay out until it was late. They were so fortunate to have found each other. It was a match made in heaven.

Harry didn't mind being there. It was better than some places she had been. At least there was no slimy grease ball demanding cheese and beans on toast every five minutes. Although, when the boys' mum came home from the pub, she often sidled up to Harry and thanked her for all the work she did, especially the cooking and cleaning. Harry didn't like it.

She didn't like the falseness of it all. If the woman cared that much, she should do it herself. Anyway, Harry didn't like the smoky beer breath.

All this was nothing new to Harry, and it certainly wasn't anything she couldn't handle. The one thing that Harry didn't like was being left in charge of the children. The two adults went out, leaving Harry to baby-sit and Harry didn't think that it was fair. Sometimes, the adults would just go out to do the shopping and they weren't gone for long. Harry didn't mind that. The boys would just carry on playing their normal rowdy games and Harry didn't have to do much to look after them. From time to time, they might fall out or have some dispute or other. Harry would let them both have their say. She listened closely and then would usually sort out the problem without too much fuss. Harry noticed that their mum would just shout at them and tell them to shut up, but that just made them get more upset and angry and generally made things worse.

Often, when Harry was left in charge, she would just sit down and watch videos with them. It was quite nice really. It was like having two little brothers to look after. Harry didn't like it so much when the two women went out for the night. The two boys had become quite adept at playing Harry up. They used to ask to stay up late. They asked for drinks of water. They asked if they could go to the toilet, over and over again. They did all of the things that any respectable children would do when they were left alone with a baby-sitter.

Harry pretended to be annoyed with them, but she never really was. They just wanted attention, some love and affection. Harry couldn't blame them for that. After all, she thought, isn't that what everybody wants?

Harry did, however, complain to the adults when they came home much later than they said they would. They didn't seem to take much notice, though, or, if they did, they didn't seem to care. Whenever they were late, all sorts of things went through her mind. She thought that they may have been run over or that they might have been attacked. Anything could have happened to them. The later they were, the more anxious Harry became. She often thought that the boys' mum was a bad influence on her own mum. Harry's mum was more than capable of getting into trouble by herself. She didn't need anybody else to lead her astray.

One night, the two women got ready to go out. They spent an age getting ready. They drank wine, listened to the radio, danced and put make-up on. In a way, it was actually quite nice. Harry was pleased to see her mum so happy. The two women had bought crisps and pop for Harry and the boys. It wasn't so bad being there.

When the adults had gone, Harry and the boys settled down to watch a video. They started on the crisps and pop. It was really nice, like being at the cinema. They were all on one settee together. One of the boys was curled up at the far end and the other was snuggled up to Harry. After a while, the boy who was snuggled up to Harry complained of feeling unwell. Harry, who had become quite used to such tactics, said, "Oh, well, then, you won't want any more pop, will you?" He just smiled and cuddled up some more. Harry thought no more of it.

A bit later he started complaining again and he sounded quite genuine. Harry felt his brow and it was warm. Harry suggested that he should go and get tucked up into bed. To her amazement, he agreed. She tucked him up and left him to settle down to sleep. She went in to check on him from time to time. He was kind of dozing. Not properly sleeping, but not really awake either. Harry felt his brow again and it was really quite warm indeed. She was quite concerned about him but she was a levelheaded girl. She wasn't about to panic.

As time went on, though, he gradually became more restless. He began calling out for his mum. Harry did her best to comfort him. She put a cold, damp cloth on his forehead and she kept telling him that it would not be too long before his mum would be home.

Harry didn't know whether she should be trying to keep him warm or cool him down. She didn't know whether to put more bedclothes on or take some off. She didn't know whether to open the windows or turn up the heat. It was a bit of a nightmare, really.

The time that the adults were due home had come and gone. Harry kept looking at the clock. She kept expecting them to walk through the door at any minute. But, time passed and there was no sign of them. Harry paced back and forth between the bedroom and the living room where she kept checking out of the window to see if they were coming home. All during this time, his brother lay asleep on the settee. Harry thought that it was best to leave him there. She didn't want to alarm or upset him. But, he became restless and started moaning and groaning. Harry went to feel his brow and he, too, was burning up. Harry told herself to keep calm. She knew that getting into a panic wasn't going to help anything. Harry helped the other little boy into bed and tucked him up as well. She gave them both lots of drinks and cold cloths for their heads but she didn't know what else to do for them. She just kept wishing that the adults would come walking through the door and take over.

The boys grew increasingly agitated. They were trying to be sick in the buckets that Harry had fetched for them and they were complaining of bad headaches. Harry decided that, if the adults did not come back soon, she was going to run down to the phone box and call for an ambulance. She didn't really want to do that because she didn't want her mum to get into any trouble for leaving them alone. She thought that she would have to, though, because the boys were getting worse by the minute. Harry became frightened. She didn't want the boys to die.

Harry waited and waited. She knew that she couldn't wait much longer. She wished that Patrick and Brian were there with her. All the time, she kept checking back at the window to see if the adults had arrived back. Harry's eyes lit up. The two women had eventually arrived home, much later than they said that they would, but at least they were home now. They stumbled out of a taxi, clutching bottles of wine. They were laughing and singing and making too much noise.

Harry ran down to meet them. She told them about everything that was happening but they obviously thought that she was over-reacting because they took no notice. The two women went straight into the front room and turned the television on. The boys' mother told Harry to shut their bedroom door and take no notice. She said that they always tried it on when she went out.

Harry went back to the boys and tried to comfort them. She gave them some more to drink and pulled their bedclothes up. They could hear that their mother had come home and they wanted to see her. Harry told them that their mother wasn't very well either, which wasn't a million miles from the truth. Harry went back to the living room to have it out with the adults, but they had both fallen asleep. The television was playing and they were both out for the count. The boys' mother was making a loud snoring and slurping noise. A kind of "thruggghhh! Flup! Flup! Flup!"

Harry decided that she couldn't wait any longer, so she went down to the corner of the street and called for an ambulance from the phone there. Harry explained what had happened, but didn't mention that the adults had gone out, leaving her alone with the boys. She thought that, if she pretended that they had been in the house all night and had just had too much to drink, they wouldn't get into trouble.

Harry went back to the flat and waited for the ambulance to come. She kept a silent vigil at the window. When the ambulance came into sight, she made the adults wake up and told them what had happened.

The rest of the night was like a dream. The adults decided not to say too much so that they wouldn't get their stories mixed up. It turned out that the boys had caught a nasty virus. They were given some medicine, which made them cool down, and, by morning, they were both sleeping comfortably.

The boys' mum realised what a debt she owed Harry and couldn't thank her enough. The next couple of weeks were something of a treat for Harry. The boys' mum couldn't do enough for her. She made meals. She didn't send her to the shops. She made her cups of tea. In fact, it was really nice. She acted like an adult and Harry was allowed to act like a child for a change.

The boys' mum said that she was never going to drink again and she was never going to leave the boys with a baby-sitter. Harry was very pleased to hear it. Although, she did say that she didn't mind looking after the boys for a while if their mum had shopping or something to do. She also said that she didn't mind having them at night, providing she knew where the adults were and she had a phone number so she could contact them, if necessary. And, most important of all, was that they would be home when they said they would be. The boys' mum wouldn't hear of it. She said that the boys were her responsibility and she wouldn't be ducking out of it again in a hurry.

This was fine for a while, but as the weeks went by, things began to slip back into their old ways. Harry was expected to do more and more about the flat and she was left alone with the boys for more and more of the time. Harry didn't really mind this, but she did mind when the adults started drinking again. At first it wasn't too much, but Harry warned them that she didn't want to be left to look after the children whilst they were drinking.

They say that leopards don't change their spots and the two adults didn't appear to have changed theirs. They gradually let their standards drop until, eventually, they came home one night, drunk, and long after they said they would be home. This was the last straw for Harry. The boys' mum had crossed her good and proper this time.

It was time for Harriet the Horrible to show herself again. Harry lay in bed that night and stroked her chin. It was a while since she had done this. It was time for her to think of a wonderfully wicked plan. She wanted one that would stop the boys' mum from taking her for granted.

"Ummmm!!" she thought to herself. "Ummmmm!!!!"

A wicked smile came over her face as she thought of the perfect plan. If this plan works, she thought, the boys' mum will not only stop taking advantage of me, she will never let me look after the boys again.

That night, she was very happy indeed as she nodded off to sleep.

Chapter Ten

Harry waited until the next time the two adults went out for a night on the town. She knew that all she had to do was wait and she was right. The boys' mum and Harry's mum had bought a new radio recently. They played it loudly as they were getting ready to go out, putting their make-up on and dancing around the room. Harry reminded them about the night that the two boys had been ill. She reminded them that they had said that they would not leave her alone with them again, in case anything went wrong.

The adults argued that it was very unlikely that something would happen again and they said that they would only be gone a few hours, anyway. Harry pointed out to them that they were taking advantage of her and that it wasn't fair. They patted her on the head and told her how good she had been the last time and how much they trusted her and all that kind of stuff to try and win her round.

Harry waved them off with a sweet smile. She knew that very soon she would be getting equal by way of one of her wonderfully wicked plans. Harry stroked her chin. She particularly liked the plan that she had in mind. With this plan everyone was a winner. The boys would be happy and Harry would be happy because, in future, the boys' mum would stop taking advantage of her.

Harry settled down with the boys to watch a video. The adults had left pop and crisps for them. Harry told the boys to share the pop because she had taken to drinking tea. The boys had just started making cups of tea for the adults. They didn't like it much. Every time they were told to make one, a fight broke out over who was going to make it. When the adults weren't there, the boys offered to make Harry a cup.

"I thought you didn't like making tea," she said to them. They said that they didn't like making it when they were ordered to, but they didn't mind making it for Harry because she was nice to them.

Harry loved snuggling up to them on the settee to watch the video. They were like the brothers that Harry had never had. When it reached their bedtime, Harry told the boys to go off to bed. They gave a token protest or two, but they soon gave Harry a hug and went off quietly enough. Sometimes, Harry forgot that she was only a couple of years older than the boys.

Harry was expecting the adults to be late and she was right. They came in very late; so late that Harry had fallen asleep on the settee. They were brushing along the wall and bumping into things. They were hiccupping and slurring their words. Harry thought that they made a very sorry picture indeed. They had won a bottle of wine in a raffle and they settled down to start on that. Harry was disgusted. She went off to bed.

The next morning, Harry jumped out of her bed with a spring in her step. She called to the boys and started a tickling fight with them. Harry picked their aeroplanes up and ran around the room making engine noises as she swung the plane round in figure-of-eights and loop-the-loops. The boys followed suit and started playing noisy games. Harry put a load of washing in the washing machine and turned it on. Then she turned the radio on good and loud. She opened the bedroom door to shout a cheery

"Good morning!" to the boys' mum. She had a face like a sleepy bulldog. She tried to speak but her tongue was too big for her mouth. When she attempted to say, "Tell the boys to be quiet for me," it came out as, "Dell de doys to de doy dor me"

Harry pulled a funny face and said that she couldn't understand. "Oh!" she said. "You want the boys to come and visit you?" Then she called the boys and told them that their mum wanted them. The boys came charging through the door and jumped on the bed.

"Hello, mum!" they shouted as they bounced up and down.

The boys' mum begged Harry to take them away. She pulled the pillow over her head and made some dying noises. Harry had a big smile on her face. Her wonderfully wicked plan was now beginning to take shape.

Harry called into the boys' mum and asked if she could have some money to take them out. Harry was told to take anything she wanted from the purse but when she looked, there was no money in there. Harry knew that the boys' mum kept money in a jar on a shelf, so

Harry asked if she could get some from there. She was told to take whatever she wanted and she was also told that she could take them out for the whole day, if she liked.

Harry duly obliged. She took all of the money from the jar and set off for a day out with the boys. The first stop they made was at the sweet shop. They all had a pocket full of sweets and chocolates and they had a can of cola each. The boys couldn't thank Harry enough. She told them not to thank her, "Your mum's paying for it," she said, and a wicked smile spread across her face.

The next stop was the amusement arcade. They went on all of the shooting games. They were the ones that the boys liked the best. They jumped off one game and straight onto another. They played the slot machines and roll a penny. They bought a huge stick of candy floss each and sat playing bingo. They wandered around the town for a while and looked in lots of shops. The boys waited on chairs whilst Harry tried on dresses. She came out of the changing room and walked up and down and did a twirl for them. After about eight dresses and as many hats, the shop assistant began to lose her cool. She asked if Harry actually intended to buy a dress and Harry said that she didn't think that she would today, after all. Harry and the boys started to giggle as they left the shop. Harry could tell that the assistant wasn't best pleased. Harry made a mental note not to go back there in a hurry.

They were all getting a little tired so they decided to go for something to eat. They stopped off at a café and ordered the works. They had burgers, chips, eggs, beans and spaghetti. They had thick milk shakes and chocolate cake with cream. It was the best nosh up they'd ever had. Harry settled the bill and left a ten pence tip for the waiter.

They walked out into the fresh air and patted their fat tummies. "Ahhhh!" said Harry. "It smells nice doesn't it?"

The boys thought that she was talking about the fresh air, but she was really talking about the sweet smell of revenge.

During the afternoon, they went to the pictures. They saw some great cartoons and a film set in space. The boys loved it. It wasn't Harry's favourite kind of film, but she was happy because the boys were happy. After the film, Harry told them that they had one more treat in store. The boys couldn't believe it. Today had already been the best day of their lives. When Harry told them that they were going to the funfair they let out a great cheer. They had never been to a fair before.

The boys were wide-eyed when they saw the fair. It was evening time and music was being played all around them. Bells were ringing and people were screaming in delight. It was a wonderful atmosphere and all three of them were soaking it up. They went on the dodgems and the waltzers. They went on the big wheel and into the hall of mirrors. They took a ride on the ghost train and screamed all the way round.

Harry bought them all hot dogs with fried onions and tomato ketchup all over them. None of them could eat them all and ended up throwing them in the bin, but it was great fun having them all the same.

It was a wonderful day and a wonderful night as well, but the night was drawing in and they were getting tired. Harry decided it was time that they went home, so she ordered a taxi. The boys had never been in a taxi before. Harry told them that she was surprised. After all, she knew that their mum used taxis. Harry had seen her often enough.

When they got home, it was to a very cold reception. The boys' mum asked where they had been. She said that she had been worried sick. She thought that anything might have happened to them. They could have been run over by a bus or they could have got into all kinds of trouble.

Harry told her that they were fine and she added that they weren't supposed to be home by any particular time anyway. The adults said that that wasn't the point because they had been worried out of their minds. They told Harry that she should have been more thoughtful because she was old enough to know better.

The adults thought that the children must have been starving. The boys' mum asked if they had eaten during the day. The boys told her about all of the things that Harry had bought them to eat. The boys' mum asked Harry where she got all the money

"You gave it to me," Harry said.

"I did? When?" the boys' mum asked.

"You gave it to me this morning. You told me to take the money out of the jar and take the boys out for the day." The boys' mum clearly had no memory of it. She looked rather shocked and went a little white as well.

The boys began to tell the adults about their day out. They told them about the pockets full of chocolate and sweets. The adults turned and looked at each other. The boys told them about their visit to the cafe and the adults grabbed hold of each other's arms. When the boys told them about the pictures, they put their hands over their ears. The boys were warming up to their tale and they began to talk about their visit to the funfair. The adults began to start pulling their hair.

"Is there any more?" the boys' mum asked.

"Yes," they said. "We came here in a taxi!"

The adults were stunned. "Exactly how much money did you take out of the jar, Harry?" the boys' mum asked.

"Oh, all of it," Harry replied politely. The boys' mum choked as she gasped for air. She made her way over to the cupboard and looked in the jar. There it was - empty!

"I don't believe it," she said. "I just don't believe it." She kept looking into the jar as though repeated observation would make it change. She paced up and down repeating it over and over again.

"I don't believe it. I just don't believe it." The boys' mum turned to Harry's mum and said, "Can you see what she's done? Can you see what your daughter's done?" Harry's mum didn't know what to say.

Harry put on her best pathetic voice. "Is there anything wrong?" she asked.

"Is there anything wrong? Is there anything wrong? Are you mad?" the boys' mum was more than a bit upset. She went on to tell Harry that she had spent all of the money that she had put aside to pay bills for the whole of next week. She said that she didn't know how she was going to pay the bills. She didn't know how they were going to eat. Harry's mum asked her why she did it. Harry said she was just doing what she was told. The boys' mum had told her to take the money out of the jar and take the boys out for the day.

The boys' mum chipped in, "Yes, but I didn't mean all of it. I meant take a pound or two and take them to the park and treat them to an ice-cream or something." Harry said that she could do that tomorrow if she wanted her to.

"You can't now, you stupid girl. You've spent every penny I've got. How much change have you got left anyway?"

Harry said that she hadn't got any change.

"Actually, I spent some of my own money, so you owe me two pound thirty eight pence." Harry said.

The boys' mum held up the jar as though she was ready to hit Harry with it. Harry's mum took it away from her. The boys' mum began pacing up and down again

"She's not staying with my boys again." The boys' mum was looking at Harry's mum, and she was pointing at Harry.

"She's a bad influence. She's irresponsible. She's got some serious growing up to do, if you ask me. And there'll be no more nights out for a long time to come. It'll be months before I'll be able to get straight from this."

Harry's mum suggested that Harry should go off to bed. It was late and tempers were raised. Harry acted as though she didn't know that she had done anything wrong. She kissed her mum on the cheek and said goodnight and went off to bed.

That night, Harry lay on her bed and thought to herself that the result of her action meant that the two adults were going to spend more time at home. Harry wasn't going to be left baby-sitting the boys on her own and she and the boys had had the day out of their lives.

"It's a funny old world," she thought. She was exceedingly tired and very contented as she fell off into a deep sleep.

Chapter Eleven

It wasn't long before Harriet and her mum moved on again. Harry missed the boys, but it was nice to get back to some kind of normality again. That's if you could call anything in Harry's life normal. Harry's mum seemed quite calm about moving on this time. She even, for a change, gave Harry a couple of days to say her goodbyes.

The new school that Harry went to seemed all right. It was quite a calm place. The Head Teacher was a little man with a bald patch and a look about him that made him seem as though he was permanently sorry for something. He had something of a twitch as though he was always afraid someone was going to tell him off. Quite often there *was* somebody who was going to tell him off. It was the school secretary. She was a most formidable woman. She wore tight tweed skirts and posh pearls around her neck. She also wore glasses on a string around her neck and, when she was wearing them, she was one of those people who peered over the top of them at you. Harry didn't take to this woman at all.

Harry had discovered that all teachers have a favourite subject and so you tended to get more of that subject when you were in their class. Her new teacher liked reading and writing, so that suited Harry fine as she loved reading and writing as well.

Harry had stopped going out of her way to make friends. She knew that it was only a matter of time before she would have to move on and it was best not to get too close to them. It was easier to leave then. She kept thinking of Patrick and Brian. They had made her life seem bright and normal. Thinking of them always made her happy.

Spring was in the air. Their new town was quiet and a bit lazy. Their new flat was a downstairs one with a garden. It was OK. It was quite a small flat, which meant that it was fairly easy for Harry to keep tidy. Though, it must be said that her mum had tidied up her act considerably since they had stayed with Patrick and Brian. Some of their tidiness had rubbed off on Harry's mum.

There was a nice winding river that ran through their town and Harry liked to walk by it. One day, Harry was walking alongside the river when she came upon a scruffy little dog. The two took to each other straight away. Harry sat down and the dog came and plonked himself down on her lap. Harry played with the dog for ages. Some children from her school came by and told her that the dog was a stray. They said he didn't have an owner and that she should be careful as the dog was vicious and he bit people.

The dog didn't seem very vicious to Harry. In fact, he seemed lovely and playful. The dog was the cleverest dog in the world. Whatever Harry asked him to do, he would do it straight away. He could sit, beg, fetch a stick and even lie down to have his tummy tickled and all on command. Harry seemed to know what the dog was thinking. He followed her home and Harry started giving him some food. Harry's mum tried to discourage it, but once she saw how inseparable they were, she soon came to accept that the dog was there to stay.

Harry called the dog Salty because he liked salt and vinegar on his chips. She could have called him tea and toast because that's what he liked for breakfast, but she called him Salty because it somehow suited him.

Harry began teaching Salty to do increasingly better tricks. She taught him to "poke his eye out". When she gave him this command, he would brush over his eye with his paw, give a little whimper and then fall on his back pretending to be dead. Salty could jump ever so high when he was jumping for food. He could even jump backward somersaults. If Harry didn't like the look of someone, she would say, "Salty, will you growl at him, please?" People used to smile when they looked at the little dog but when Salty bared his teeth and growled, people soon changed the look on their face. People would walk on the other side of the road when they saw Harry and Salty approach. Harry loved her new friend.

Harry came to look upon Salty as a very special friend because he didn't belong anywhere. He was a stranger just like Harry. They belonged together. Harry explained to him that one day she would have to move on. She told him that she thought her mum was in some kind of trouble but she didn't know quite what it was. Salty seemed to understand.

Harry had lots of fun with Salty. She bought a dog whistle. It made a noise that was too high pitched for humans to hear but Salty could hear from a long way away. It meant that Harry could give Salty commands that no one else could hear. It was brilliant.

One day, when they were walking down the high street, Harry went into the butcher's shop to get some meat for Salty. Salty sneaked in by her side. When the butcher's back was turned, Salty put his paws up on the counter and grabbed a sausage in his teeth. Harry could see that he was going to pull the whole tray off, so she shouted, "STOP!"

The butcher looked round and so Harry quickly said, "Stop buzzing around, you naughty fly," and she started jumping up and pretending to catch a fly that wasn't there. The butcher gave Harry a rather strange look and then turned back to continue doing what he was doing before. Harry picked up the string of sausages very quietly and was about to feed them to Salty when the butcher turned round again and caught them red-handed.

"Oh heck, Salty. It's time to leave," she said. Harry and Salty ran out of the shop as quickly as they could. Salty had the string of sausages in his mouth.

"Stop that dog! And that naughty girl! They've stolen my best sausages!" He was waving a big chopping knife as he ran down the road after them.

Harry and Salty ran down the high street and people jumped out of their way when they saw them coming. They ran down a side street and jumped over garden fences. Harry ran into some washing and a sheet covered her head and arms. She looked like a ghost running down the road. Harry flung the sheet off and carried on running.

She shouted to passers-by, "Help! Help! There's a mad axe man chasing us. Help! Help!" One kind passer-by heard this and stepped in front of the butcher.

"You should be ashamed of yourself," the man said. "A grown man like you chasing a little girl like that, and with an axe as well!"

The butcher was puffing and panting, "You don't understand," he said. "She and that dog are in it together. They've stolen my best sausages."

By this time, Harry and her dog had got too far away for the butcher to catch them. Harry looked back at him, she put her thumbs in her ears, wiggled her fingers and stuck her tongue out. The butcher knew that he was too out of breath to catch them. He shook his fist and shouted, "I'll get you one day. Don't you ever come near my shop again!" He caught his breath before continuing, "If I ever lay eyes on you again, young lady, I'll take you to the police and they can sort you out!"

Harry went home happily and Salty ate his sausages. They were the best kind.

Chapter Twelve

During a pretty boring maths lesson, Harry was half listening and half day dreaming as she stared out of the window. Their classroom was on the second floor and so Harry had a good view of the playground. Often the secretary would walk across the playground from one side of the school to the other. She had a snooty kind of gait. You could tell, even by the way that she walked, that she thought she was a cut above everybody else.

The secretary had got into the habit of shouting at Harriet for coming into school late. She had called the Head Teacher over once and told him to tell Harry off as well. The Head Teacher, who was obviously afraid of the secretary, said that it was really her mother's fault and perhaps they should have a word with her.

"Oh, Headmaster," the secretary said, "Sometimes you are really useless. Do you know that? You run along to class, Harriet, and make sure you come into school on time tomorrow. Headmaster, you had better go and write some letters or something. You had better do something that you can do properly."

"Er, well, yes, OK, then," the Headmaster replied rather sheepishly. "I'll just pop along to my office then."

Harry felt quite sorry for him. She didn't usually feel that sorry for Head Teachers.

Perhaps it was time for Harriet to pull her down a peg or two. As Harry watched her mincing along the playground in her high heels and her tight little tweed skirt, with her posh pearls around her neck, a little smile crept across Harry's face. Harry stroked her chin. Hmmmm! she thought to herself. I've just thought of a wonderfully wicked plan.

Harry got out her dog whistle and called for Salty. Humans couldn't hear the high-pitched sound of the whistle. The teacher was still droning on about some weary old maths or something, but Harry was going to have a lot more fun than listening to her.

Harry waited until the secretary came back out into the playground and then she started blowing her commands to Salty. Salty made his way towards the secretary and started growling at her. She inched away from him and stood still. Then she took a step to the side but Salty took a step to stop her and he growled at her some more.

Gradually, more children from the class looked out of the window. It looked as though Salty and the school secretary were having a little dance. One step to the right...one step to the left... one step to the right... one step to the left. The children were finding it most amusing.

The school secretary was looking all around her. She was too proud to call for help, which made it look all the funnier. Salty began to move round her just like a sheep dog rounding up the flock. Then he crouched down on his front paws and growled even louder.

"Oh dear!" she shouted as she tried to run away, but she found it very difficult to run on her high heels. "Oh dear! Oh dear!" she cried and Salty barked at her.

"Oooh!" she cried and she tried to run away some more, but a heel broke off her shoe and her hair fell down over her face. She picked up her shoe and tried to balance along with one foot up and one foot down.

Salty barked again. "Oooh heck!" she said. She took her other shoe off and tried to hobble along in her stockinged feet. Salty chased her up against a wall. He pinned her to it for a while, not letting her run this way or that. When she finally made a run for it, she stood on a stone that made her do a Red Indian dance. Her pearls fell from around her neck and made her slip and slide as they bounced down the hill. Her feet went up in the air in front of her and she landed with a big bump on the ground. She staggered to her feet and rubbed her bottom, which was obviously very sore. The whole class had gathered by the window now and were cheering Salty's every move. Even the teacher had gone to the window to see what all of the fuss was about and even she could not disguise her delight at seeing the school secretary getting her comeuppance.

Salty started barking ferociously and jumping up and down.

"Oh no!" the secretary cried as she jumped and skipped in an effort to get away. She ran to a tree and tried to climb it. She clung onto one of the branches and tried to hurl herself free from him by throwing her leg over the branch, but Salty jumped right behind her.

"Agggghhh!" she cried.

All of the children gave out the biggest cheer of their lives.

"Aggghhhggghhh!!!" the secretary cried again. "That mangy brute has got half of my knickers in his mouth. Help! Help! Somebody help!"

When the Head Teacher came out, Salty had gone and the school secretary was stuck up the tree.

"Come here at once," she shouted to him. "Get me down from this tree at once."

The Head Teacher didn't quite know what to make of it all.

"Give me your jacket now," she demanded. "Avert your eyes whilst I climb down from this tree."

She tied the jacket around her waist to cover her bare bottom and marched into school. She shouted back at the Head Teacher, "This is all your fault. If you weren't such a lily-livered, spineless, sorry excuse of a man, none of this would have happened."

The Head Teacher just stood and pointed to himself. "Me?" he whimpered. "What have I done?"

She shouted back some more, "And pick those pearls up before you come in!" As she walked into school she could be heard shouting, "And what do you think you're looking at? Have you never seen a bare footed woman with a man's jacket around her waist before?" Everybody could hear her slamming doors as she marched back to her office.

Harriet couldn't wait to meet up with Salty after school. He had been superb.

That night, Harry lay in bed thinking about the wonderful show that they had put on for everybody. Salty slept on the bed next to Harry. He licked her face before they both went off to sleep.

Chapter Thirteen

Playing the school secretary up had become a favourite pastime for Harry. She was so easy. She was so pompous and ridiculous and loud, but most of all she was, by nature, a bully. She brought out the most wicked of wonderfully wicked plans in Harry.

During a science lesson, another wonderfully wicked plan popped into Harry's mind. The children were all dissecting dead mice to find out all about their insides. The secretary walked into their classroom and nearly fainted. She looked away and put the back of her hand in front of her eyes.

"Oh. Why didn't somebody tell me that you had mice in here? They're revolting little creatures. Ugghh!! They're disgusting. Get me out of here."

Oh dear, thought Harry, the poor secretary doesn't like mice! What a shame. If she feels faint at the sight of a dead mouse, I wonder how she would react if she were to see a real live mouse walking around her office? Harry stroked her chin. Hmmmm!, she thought.

This is a simple little plan but nonetheless wonderful and wicked.

Harry stopped off at the pet shop on her way home and bought a couple of nice, young, playful mice. She explained to Salty that they weren't pets and that very soon she would be giving them back to the pet shop. Harry didn't take them straight to school. Instead, she decided that it would be much more fun to make the secretary think that there might be a mouse around for a few days before she actually got to see one.

Harry collected some of the mouse droppings from the bottom of the cage and took them to school. She bided her time until there was nobody about and then she sprinkled the droppings at the side of the secretary's desk.

Even Harry could not have been prepared for the commotion that this was to cause. When the secretary went into her office and noticed the droppings, she nearly had a blue fit.

"Headmaster!" she bellowed. "Headmaster, come here at once! Look! Look!" she said, pointing at the droppings. "We've got mice! Mice! In our school! And in, of all places,

– MY OFFICE!!! Find them, Headmaster. Find them now and get rid of them, and that's an order!"

The poor old Headmaster looked a little flustered. He didn't quite know what to do. He started picking up files and moving pieces of paper around.

"Oh, for heaven's sake!" the secretary trumpeted. "You're useless, absolutely useless. I'll call my husband. He's had to deal with mice in his shop before."

The school secretary called her husband and he quickly made his way over to the school. When he arrived, Harry could not believe her eyes. It turned out that the school secretary's husband was none other than the butcher who had chased her and Salty all through the village. Harry kept her head down and made sure that she was well out of sight.

The butcher started moving desks and cupboards about, banging and clattering as he went. He stormed in this direction and that, shouting, "Come out, come out. Come on, show yourselves. I'll catch you, you little horrors. Come and show yourselves."

First of all, he stormed about his wife's office. The school secretary stood with her arms folded. She had an altogether superior look on her face as she told everybody that her husband was an expert and that he could find the mouse where the Headmaster failed. Her husband continued to throw papers this way and that. He lifted up carpets and prised up the floorboards. In the end, he fell back and sat against the wall. He was sweating and red faced.

"I'm terribly sorry, my sweet," he said. "I'm afraid I can't find him anywhere."

"You useless man," she shouted at him. "You can't even find a little mouse and just look at all of this mess that you've made! Straighten it up and get yourself home. You are useless. I'll be having words with you later!"

The poor old butcher; Harry actually felt sorry for him, even though he had chased her down the high street wielding an axe!

Harry couldn't wait for the next turn of events. She lay in bed stroking Salty and told him how much she was looking forward to seeing the secretary's expression when she came face to face with her mice.

The school secretary was humming a little tune to herself as she pottered about her office. Harry liked the calm that had descended upon the school. The secretary had clearly relaxed from the trauma of seeing the mouse droppings, so Harry decided it was time to liven things up a bit. When the secretary's back was turned, Harry left her mice in the office and then retreated to a safe distance. Harry waited outside the office and looked in through the window. And, sure enough, within a few seconds, the whole school heard about the secretary's little visitors.

"Agghh!!! Agghh!!!" they all heard.

Harry had never heard screams like it.

"Agghhh!! Help! Help! They're back! They're back! Somebody get help!" she yelled.

The mice wandered about the office, walking over the desk and the cupboards without a care in the world. The secretary was stood up on a chair in the corner of the room. She had taken off one of her high-heeled shoes and was holding it as a weapon in her hand.

After several minutes of screaming and ranting, the school secretary made a run for it. She ran down the corridor shouting, "Get out!

Get out! Everybody get out! We're being overrun with mice."

The children and teachers hurled themselves into a blind panic. There were people running this way and that and bumping into each other. The Head Teacher stood raising his arms telling people not to panic, but they took no notice of him. They just knocked him over in their rush to get out.

People were stepping on benches and running over tables. They were looking all around the floor as they scurried back and forth. Two teachers were walking up the corridor bent double to look under radiators as they went. They kept on walking until they bumped into each other's heads.

"Ow! Ow!" they shouted as they rubbed their heads better.

As all of this panic was going on, Harry calmly walked into the secretary's office and retrieved the mice. She slipped them into her pocket and, when all of the panic died down and they were sent home, Harry took them back to the pet shop. She said that she liked them but that she already had one pet at home and that was enough for her.

Perhaps it was because the secretary was so pompous that playing her up was so enjoyable. When most people are brought down a peg or two, they usually begin to see the error of their ways. They would normally begin to show a little humility, but not this lady. She just carried on in her usual pompous and arrogant way.

Harry had read a book where somebody wanting to get even with someone who had crossed them put a dead fish under the floorboards. As the fish began to rot, the smell became unbearable but no one could work out where the smell was coming from.

Harry stroked her chin. What a lovely sight that would make, she thought, our posh school secretary on her hands and knees trying to locate the source of the smell. Somehow the thought was just too irresistible for her. Harry loved the idea of it. This plan, although not strictly speaking all her own work, was wonderful and it was wicked and it was just too good an opportunity to miss.

There was an old safe in the secretary's office that hadn't been used for many years. This was the perfect place for Harry to leave her present. Harry went to the fishmongers and bought a beautiful big wet fish. She sneaked it into school and slid it into the old safe. Harry locked the door and hid the key. All she had to do was to sit back and wait for nature to take its course.

From time to time, Harry popped her head around the door of the office. Harry had to fight hard to contain her laughter when she saw the secretary giving little sniffs in the air as though she could smell a faint odour but she wasn't quite sure where it was coming from.

Gradually, the secretary called other people into her room and they too sniffed the air and tried to guess what the smell was. They all agreed that it was getting stronger.

Soon the smell became so bad that it was beginning to linger on the school secretary herself. As she walked around school, people began to pull away from her as she passed. The children held their noses when she approached. She didn't like it one little bit.

"It's not me," she said. "It's something in my office."

The scene that followed over the next few days was altogether more sedate than the incident with the mice but none the less destructive for that. One by one, people trooped into her office and offered her advice. But no solution came. The smell just got worse and worse.

The school secretary had developed a nervous twitch. She said that somebody was out to get her. She said that she meant to find out who it was and that she would get to the bottom of it. She looked at everybody through beady eyes. She suspected everybody of plotting to get her. Whenever anybody came into her office she asked them if they knew anything about the awful smell.

She took to doing her work with a huge peg on her nose. She could be heard talking to her husband on the phone, "Dumbody's dout do det me. I'll find em, I'll det em. I'll dort dem out!" What she was trying to say was, of course, "Somebody's out to get me. I'll find them. I'll get them. I'll sort them out!"

As the days went by, and the smell became worse, the school secretary became convinced that somebody was going to attack her. She took to looking over her shoulder from side to side, convinced that somebody was going to jump out at her at any minute. She carried a rounders bat everywhere she went for protection. She had bought an old World War II gas mask from a junk shop. She wore it all day in school, from the minute she arrived to the minute she went home in the evenings. When she took the gas mask off at the end of the school day, Harry said to her, "You know, Miss, you've changed so much since I first came to this school!"

The secretary screwed up her eyes and peered at Harry suspiciously. Harry gave her one of her sweet little smiles in return.

Harry decided that even the nasty old school secretary had suffered enough by now so she opened up the safe and threw the fish out.

That night, Harry lay in her bed stroking Salty and she felt particularly well pleased with herself. She liked the power that she felt when a wonderfully wicked plan worked and she liked having the power to let people off when she had got even with them.

Harry was especially contented as she went to sleep that night.

Chapter Fourteen

Whatever it was that made her mum need to leave home and move to a new area had started up again. Harry found herself on a train in the middle of the night going to a place she had never been to before. Most kids would be frightened stiff at the prospect but Harry had become used to it.

Her mum was smoking in a carriage that said no smoking. There was a man who coughed a bit and patted his chest. Harry's mum took no notice. In the end, the man coughed loudly and pointed to the no smoking sign. Harry's mum coughed back and stood up and turned her bottom towards him and she pointed at that. Harry was amused. She made a mental note that she should do that herself one day.

Harry's mum asked her for some money, but Harry told her that she didn't have any. Her mum didn't believe her so Harry had to turn out her pockets. Her mum still didn't believe her so she said that she would turn Harry upside down and shake her until some money dropped out. Harry protested some more. The man sitting opposite joined in, saying that a grown woman shouldn't treat a young girl like that.

Harry could tell that her mum was really angry. Harry told her that she really didn't have any money and her mum reluctantly believed her. Her mum huffed and puffed and tossed and turned in her seat for a bit and then said that she was going for a walk. And with that she stormed off down the train.

The man sitting across from Harry came and sat next to her and asked her if she was all right. Harry kicked him in the shin and he hurriedly returned to his seat.

When Harry's mum came back she was shaking and sweating. She put her fingers to her lips. She whispered to her daughter to be quiet and told her to come along down the train in the other direction. Harry asked her mum what the matter was. Her mum told her that it was nothing for her to worry about. Of course, Harry said that she was already worried. She demanded that her mum tell her what it was that had frightened her. Her mum said that it was nothing that need concern her and that she didn't need this right now and that was that.

Harry's mum bundled her into a toilet and the two of them pushed up together so that her mum could lock the door. Her mum told her that they would get out and make a run for it at the next station. Harry asked her mum where the next station was, but her mum didn't know. Harry decided that she would be better off not asking any more questions. After a while, an announcement came over the loudspeaker saying that the train was now approaching the next station and that they would arrive there in approximately five minutes.

Harry's mum was shaking worse than ever. She told Harry to promise that, whatever happened in the next five minutes, she was to remember that her mum loved her and always would. Harry promised, but it made her more frightened than ever. It was the not knowing that hurt more than anything.

When the train pulled into the station, Harry and her mum came out of the toilet and they jumped off the train, making a dash for a big pillar and hiding behind it. Harry's mum put her back up against the pillar and took some deep breaths. Harry clung on to her tightly. As the train pulled out, Harry's mum peered around the corner and searched all of the carriages as they passed. It was the middle of the night and so there weren't too many people on the train.

Harry's mum began to allow a smile to creep over her face. She had a quick look up and down the platform and decided that the coast was clear. Harry's mum stepped out from the shadows and saw a man who was standing on the other side of the pillar.

Harry's mum let out an enormous scream and backed away from him. She shouted at him to stay away from her and her daughter, "Stay away! Stay away from us!" she screamed.

The man stepped forward and said, "But I only wanted to see your ticket, love."

Harry's mum breathed a sigh of relief. It was only the ticket collector. Harry's mum started laughing and crying at the same time. She gave the man her tickets. He told her that she should still be on the train, but Harry's mum told him there had been a change of plan.

The two of them walked off into the town. Harry's mum had no money, so finding somewhere to sleep was going to be difficult.

They wandered around for a while until they finally lay down on a bench outside a pavilion in a park. Harry was so exhausted that she fell asleep straight away but she kept waking up every few minutes. Harry's mum was still awake. Her mum stroked her hair and told her to go back to sleep.

Harry was missing Salty. Her mum had made her leave him behind. Salty seemed to understand. It wasn't like he really belonged to Harry. He didn't belong anywhere really. Harry missed him so much she thought her heart would burst every time she thought of him. He was her best friend ever. She thought of Patrick and Brian and her eyes filled with tears as she drifted back to sleep.

Harry's mum, it seemed, was losing her knack of finding somewhere to stay. The council offered them a place for the night but Harry's mum said that it didn't seem safe enough. They walked around all day and went back to their bench in the park for a second night. The night was long and cold and, by morning, Harry's mum had made a momentous decision. She decided to head off for London where she had heard that the streets were paved with gold.

True enough, things were better there, but only just. They found a flat to stay in. It was in a high-rise block but many of the flats had been boarded up and nobody lived there. There were smoke stains on the side of building where there had obviously been a lot of fires.

Harry hated it there. There were parties every night with loud music and people shouting to each other. Some nights she could hear screaming from the streets below and police and fire engine sirens wailing.

The local school was a disgrace. She made no friends, but, as far as she could make out, nobody had any friends there. Strangely enough there were no gangs there. Everybody was on their own. It was horrible for Harry because nobody new ever came to the school so she was an outsider amongst outsiders. She wouldn't even think of coming up with one of her wonderfully wicked plans. It was too dangerous. She was in a place where mad people pretend not to be mad. Her mum started drinking heavily. She took to staying in at night worrying. Harry wished that there were something she could do to help. She would love to be able to keep her mum safe so that she didn't have to worry about anything ever again.

Harry decided to wag it from school to get some money for her mum. She told her mum that she was going to school but instead went to an underground station and started begging.

Harry and her mum had been given beds and a TV by the council but one day Harry came home to find that her mum had sold the TV so that she could buy some more drink.

This was the bottom. They had nowhere left to fall. Things carried on like this for too long until Harry came home one day to find that her mum was washed and dressed and smiling. She was looking happy. Harry had forgotten what this looked like. Harry's mum said that she had the best news. She put her arms around Harry and told her it was all over. She said that they could go home at last and that there would be no more moving on.

Harry couldn't believe it; at first it was like waking up from a bad dream. They packed their possessions, such as they were, and left for the station. This time it was better than ever. They walked slowly from their flat. Harry's mum told everyone that she met where they were going. She said that it felt good to be able to tell everybody because they weren't running away anymore. They were going home!

Harry's mum found out that their old house was empty and they were able to move back in. It was still a tip, but it was their tip and Harry had never been so pleased to see any sight in her life.

When she got back to her old school she couldn't wait to meet up with Miss Short. Miss Short had missed her just as much as Harry had missed her old teacher. It was great to meet up with all her old friends again.

At last Harry felt at home - where she belonged at last! When she walked home from school, after her first day back, she felt a warm safe glow all over. Harry and her mum were home at last. It was a great feeling. Harry's mum had promised her that all of their problems were behind them. They were safe now and they would always be safe from now on. Harry believed her and it was a wonderful feeling.

When she arrived home, she found that a lot of the rubbish had been removed from the front of the house. She walked inside to find that her mum had overalls on and was giving the place a spring clean. Harry could hear sounds upstairs. Harry's mum told her that she had a little surprise for her.

"OK," she called up the stairs. "She's home. You can come down now!"

Harry jumped for joy when Patrick and Brian came down the stairs. They swung her around in their arms and gave her lots of hugs and kisses. Patrick and Brian had come to help them settle in and they promised that they would be regular visitors from now on. They also told Harry that she must promise to visit them. It was the happiest day of her life.

The adults carried on working and Harry cooked them a lovely meal. Patrick and Brian were going to be around for several more days but they had to stay in a hotel because Harry's mum had only managed to acquire one bed so far.

Harry and her mum lay in bed together that night and Harry felt happier than she could ever have imagined. Harry thought to herself that you could only really experience true happiness when you've experienced real sadness.

Harry could hear a noise outside. It was someone moving about. Her mum went rigid with fright. It was very strange. Harry's mum picked up a hammer and went to investigate. Her mum opened the front door and shouted out, "How did you find us? How did you know where we were? I didn't think we'd ever see you again!"

Harry went rushing to the door and, when she got there, she was shocked to see Salty, standing there wagging his tail.

"Salty! Salty!" she cried. "You've come home with us! You clever boy!" She knelt down and hugged and stroked him. He jumped all over her and licked her face. Harry kept calling him a clever boy. They had no idea how he had managed to find them, but they were delighted that he had.

Harry made Salty tea and toast after his long journey and the three of them went up to bed. Harry's mum let him sleep on the end of the bed, but she drew the line at letting him get into it with them.

They lay quietly for a while and Harry told her mum that she never wanted to talk about the past. She said that she wanted to put it behind them, but before she did, she needed to know what it was that had made them keep on the road for so long. Harry's mum held her close. She said that there were some things that children should never get to know about and that was that.